Here's what teens are saying about Bluford High:

"As soon as I finished one book, I couldn't wait to start the next one. No books have ever made me do that before."
—Terrance W.

"The suspense got to be so great I could feel the blood pounding in my ears."
—Yolanda E.

"Once I started reading them, I just couldn't stop, not even to go to sleep."
—Brian M.

"Great books! I hope they write more."
—Eric J.

"When I finished these books, I went back to the beginning and read them all over again. That's how much I loved them."
—Caren B.

"I found it very easy to lose myself in these books. They kept my interest from beginning to end and were always realistic. The characters are vivid, and the endings left me in eager anticipation of the next book."
—Keziah J.

BLUFORD HIGH

Lost and Found

A Matter of Trust

Secrets in the Shadows

Someone to Love Me

The Bully

Payback

Until We Meet Again

Blood Is Thicker

Brothers in Arms

Summer of Secrets

The Fallen

Shattered

Search for Safety

No Way Out

Schooled

Breaking Point

The Test

Pretty Ugly

Brothers in Arms

PAUL LANGAN
AND BEN ALIREZ

Series Editor: Paul Langan

SCHOLASTIC INC.

New York Toronto London Auckland
Sydney Mexico City New Delhi Hong Kong

ISBN 978-0-439-90490-2

12 11   11 12 13 14 15 16/0

Printed in the U.S.A.   23

First Scholastic printing, January 2008

Chapter 1

I'm standing in front of Bluford High School, blood on my elbows, gash on my head. My ribs feel cracked. The school is crowded, and I'm three hours late.

I wish I could cut again.

Ms. Spencer, our school principal, will bust me for sure if I go in now. She's heard enough from the other teachers about me, Martin Luna, the dangerous kid from the barrio who used to go to Zamora High. Last time I was in her office, she just stared at me, judging me, her eyes beaming like a cop's spotlight.

"What's the problem between you and Steve Morris?" she asked.

"Nothin'," I said. Even though I hate the kid, I ain't a rat.

She crossed her arms and sighed, still looking at me as if I was some kind a puzzle. I could see she was losing patience. I don't blame her. I ain't easy to deal with. Still, I stared back at her until she was forced to look away. You can't stare me down. I've been hit by people who would scare you on the street. I don't run from anyone, not principals or kids like Steve Morris who give me trouble. That's part of my problem.

But I ran this morning. I bolted like the roaches in the basement of our old apartment when you turned the light on them. Back in the day, me and my brother would chase them into the shadows, though Huero would never stomp them like me. He was always a good kid. I miss him so much.

What I ran from wasn't no kid. It wasn't the police or a gang. It was bigger than that, and I am not sure running is even gonna save me. And all I got right now is this school that can't handle me and the words my English teacher, Mr. Mitchell, said yesterday.

"Martin, you are talented, and you could have a bright future ahead of you. Don't throw it away. When you feel things getting out of hand, when you know you're getting over your head, talk to me. I'm here for you. I mean that."

I shrugged off his words when he said them. But now I'm hoping they're true, 'cause I feel like I'm bein' swept away. I'm over my head. I realized it this morning, but it's been happening for months, years actually. Now I gotta make a choice.

I see the security guard at the door watching me. He's talking to someone on a radio. Ms. Spencer is on her way out to me. This is it.

What should I do?

All this started on July 10th. I remember exactly what happened because I still dream about it. Sometimes I wake up in the middle of the night covered in sweat, my heart jumping against my ribs. I'm never gonna forget.

Me and my four homeboys were hanging out in the alley behind my friend Frankie's house. We were watching him wax his 1972 Pontiac LeMans. Chrome wheels and as blue as the ocean, the car was Frankie's baby. If you asked him, he'd say he treated it better than any person. It's true.

The southern California sun was beating down on us, making the concrete

3

so hot the bottoms of our shoes got soft and sticky, but we had music from the car stereo. And Chago, one of our boys, had a case of beer. I never drank the stuff because I saw what it did to my father, and what he did when he was drunk, but Chago was different. He liked his beer, and he didn't get too out of hand, so it was all good.

We were just kicking it, talking cars and girls, when Frankie looked at me and Chago.

"Homies, I gotta find me a chick. I spend way too much time with you low-lifes," Frankie said.

We laughed. Frankie Pacheco was the toughest guy in our crew. He also got in the most trouble. There were lots of rumors about things Frankie had done, but he never talked about them unless he was drunk, and then you couldn't listen to him. A scar on his left side marked where someone had stabbed him last summer. I was there that day backing him up. I watched Frankie kick the kid with the knife in the stomach and face. Frankie knew how to handle himself. He was nineteen, three years older than me. Other people might've had problems with him. But we thought he was family.

"Dude, you're dreaming," I teased, throwing a light punch his way. "You ever look in the mirror?"

Junie cracked up and nearly spit out a mouthful of beer onto Frankie's car. He was always laughing at something.

Frankie punched me right back, the hit glancing off my shoulder. The two of us always pretended to fight. Though we never said anything about it, I think we both knew there was a serious edge to it.

"Hey, Martin," said Jesus, one of the other guys. He was puffing a cigarette. It made him stink like my father. "I got Huero at 11:00."

I swung around in time to see a small figure ducking behind a green metal dumpster the size of a pickup truck. It was Huero, my eight year old brother. Huero's real name was Eric. Huero was just his nickname, a Spanish word that means *light-skinned*. We called him that since he was a little kid 'cause his skin was paler than mine and my mom's.

"He's back *again*?" Frankie asked, shaking his head and dropping his fists. Frankie didn't like many things, especially kids. "I don't know *nobody* who worships someone like that little brother

5

of yours worships you."

It was true. Huero had a habit of following me, no matter where I was or what I was doing. It was frustrating and I tried to discourage it. I mean, how do you deal with someone who looks up to you like, well, like a big brother?

I wasn't always the best at dealing with him, but I didn't want him around, especially when we were drinking or checking out girls. It isn't cool to have your little brother there when you're trying to get a girl's phone number. And I didn't want him around the cigarettes and the alcohol. He would see that on his own in a few years, I thought. I was wrong.

"Make sure you take care of your brother," my mom said earlier that day. Most of the time, I did that by sending him away, making up lies to get him to leave. Anything that gave me more time with the boys.

"Huero!" I barked, stepping away from Frankie's lowrider. "Come out of there."

Huero came out from behind the dumpster a second later, pushing along his squeaky, weather-beaten bicycle. He took that bike everywhere.

"What did I tell you about following me?"

"Sorry, Marty," he stammered. "I just—"

"You just what?" I prodded. "You know you're not supposed to be here."

With puppy-dog eyes, he looked over at the boys and ignored me. "Hi, guys, I got some gum. I can share it with you."

Chago and Frankie shook their heads at me and glanced away embarrassed.

"Go home, Huero—*now!*" I ordered.

My brother stared at me then. Just for a second, but long enough for me to see his disappointment. All the kid wanted was to be with me, and there I was sending him away.

"Okay, Marty," he said, sounding defeated. "I'll see you later then, okay?"

"Yeah, yeah," I said with a nod, feeling guilty for chasing him away. I couldn't stay mad at Huero for long. And no matter how bad I treated him, he just kept coming back to me with those eyes. The kid looked at me like I was a superhero or something. *Me.* He was too young to know better.

I watched him for a second as he began to pedal away, and then I turned around. "Brothers! Did I tell you guys what he said this morning?" I asked.

"What's that?"

"Huero said he wants to be just like me when he gets older. Can you believe that?" The idea seemed silly to me then. Now it haunts me.

We all laughed, but then we heard Huero shouting in the distance.

"*Marty!*"

I turned back to see him pedaling my way as fast as he could.

A half block behind him, a white sedan was speeding down the alley in our direction. Something was sticking out of the window. It glinted in the bright sunlight.

"Watch out, Marty," Huero yelled. My little brother was trying to protect *me*.

The car raced toward us, its windshield tinted so I couldn't get a good look inside. Huero was pedaling fast, but the car was coming faster. I yelled for him to get out of the way, but he wasn't rushing for cover. He could have hid behind the dumpster, or he could have darted to the side of the street. But instead Huero came toward me, his big brown eyes wide open and unblinking as he pedaled, the bike squeaking like a field of crickets.

Chago, Jesus, and Frankie were scrambling behind the lowrider. I could hear their shoes scraping the concrete.

"Get down, homes!" Frankie yelled.

Then the shots rang out.

Pop! Pop! Pop! They sounded like loud firecrackers, but the smell was different, more crisp, like the smell of burning matches. The kind that burns the inside of your nose.

Huero reached me, leaping from his bike into my arms as the car approached. I didn't have time to think. I just grabbed him and turned so that my body covered his like a shield.

More shots rang out. A bullet zinged past my ear. Another hit the sidewalk and rocketed into a window somewhere. I can still hear the glass breaking in my dreams. Then, just as suddenly, the bullets stopped. Looking back over my shoulder, I saw the car turning the corner, its wheels squealing like some kind of demon.

"They're gone, dude," said Frankie. He stepped out from behind the Le Mans.

My heart was about to jump out of my chest. I'd heard gunshots, and I'd seen a store after a shooting. But I'd never been shot at before. I took a deep breath when I was sure they were gone.

"It's okay now, Huero." I said. My little brother looked like he was sleeping. I almost didn't want to bother him. "Huero?" I repeated.

The guys rushed to my side as I remained kneeling.

"Come on little buddy, wake up. What's the matter?" I put my arm under him to sit him up, and I felt the wetness in my hand. It was warm, like bathwater, but it was coming out the back of his head.

"Martin, it don't look like he's breathing," Chago said softly. The tone of his voice alarmed me 'cause Chago never talked like that.

"Oh, no," Junie said.

My vision was breaking up like I was seeing the world through shattered glass. My hands were red, and my little brother's life was spilling out onto the street, mixing with the soil like rain.

This wasn't happening. It couldn't be. Not to my brother.

"Come on, Huero," I said, rocking him like I did when he was little. "Come on."

People were starting to gather around,

but I blocked them out. Huero was going to wake up. He had to.

I touched his cheek. He was still warm, and his skin was soft like when he was a baby. But my fingers left smudges of blood on his face, and his body was limp. "Wake up for your big brother," I said. "Wake up!"

A woman screamed in the crowd behind me, and then I heard a voice.

"Call an ambulance! That boy's been shot."

I couldn't talk or move or think. I just sat there on the ground holding my little brother.

Someone put an arm on my shoulder. I turned to see Frankie there, his eyes dark and stormy, his brow rumpled like a dented car.

"We'll get them, homes," he said. "We'll get them." He patted me on the shoulder and walked away. I heard the sirens screaming closer then.

I couldn't let go of Huero when the medics arrived. They had to pull me away because I wasn't going to give up on my little brother. But inside, I knew he was gone. And, in a way, so was I.

Whoever shot him tore a hole through my heart too, a black hole that, instead of blood, gushed only a desire for revenge. And as I endured the trip to the hospital, the sound of my mother wailing at the top of her lungs, the sight of my brother's blood spilling into the sink when I washed my hands, that desire grew like a tumor.

That was two months ago.

Chapter 2

"Don't do it, *mijo*. Don't try to get even," my mom said when we got home from burying my brother. She almost always called me *mijo*, especially when she was upset. It's the Spanish word for *son*.

My mom is smart. She knew I wanted revenge. She could see it my eyes, in the tight-jawed look I gave my friends.

I turned away from her.

"Look at me, Martin," she pleaded, tears in her eyes. "Tell me that you won't, and I'll believe you."

"Ma, don't—"

"Tell me!" she demanded, her voice breaking up.

I couldn't stand to see her crying. I'd seen it too much in my life. When I was a kid, she sobbed when my dad drank too much and started hitting. Then, after he left at Huero's birth, she cried for days. I could sometimes hear her in her bedroom weeping late into the night. She tried to hide the sound with pillows, but I knew what she was doing.

Yet when Huero died, she wailed louder than ever before. Even when she managed to stop, there were quiet tears rolling from her eyes, sparkling on her face like tiny shards of broken glass.

"I won't, Ma," I assured her. But I lied.

Whenever we could, me, Frankie, Junie, Chago, and Jesus would roll out in the Le Mans and look for that white sedan. We spent summer afternoons cruising slowly through neighborhoods filled with brown Chicano kids who looked just like us. They watched us warily as we passed by, the same way we kept an eye on people who drove down our street.

"We'll get 'em, Martin. Don't you worry, homes," Frankie said. He had bought a gun, a 9-millimeter pistol, which he kept hidden in a pocket on the underside of the front bench seat. No one could see it, but we all knew it was there. I knew if it came down to it and we found the people in that car, I'd be the one to pull the trigger. I would do it for Huero. Even if I couldn't save him, I could take out the one who took him. That's just the way it goes down on the street. I'd heard about it all my life, and now I was becoming it. A gangbanger.

In the weeks after the funeral, I started hanging out even more with Frankie and his friends. There were a few parties, people smoking and getting high. It wasn't my thing, but I was changing with Huero gone. I didn't want to be home to see his empty room, his toys, his pictures everywhere, even the one he drew of me and Frankie and the Le Mans on the refrigerator. Mom used magnets to hold the drawing in place. One of them was a tiny photo of Huero in his Little League uniform. I loved that kid.

My mom put some candles and a rosary around a picture of him in the corner of her bedroom. It was like having a little church in our home, but it just made me angrier. What good are prayers when your brother is already dead?

One night Frankie said he had something special for me. We were at this kid Oscar's house. It was late. There was a bunch of people I knew from my school, Zamora High. Some were older than me, people who dropped out, but there were others I didn't know. Frankie led me to the backyard. There must have been fifty people standing around. Some girls were dancing while guys were checking them out. Other people sat in groups drinking and laughing. The music was loud.

"Check this out, homes. He's joining the family."

As I watched, a kid my age stepped forward and everybody formed a circle around him. Then five other guys jumped him. They punched and kicked the kid, who did little to defend himself except raise his hands to protect his head. He tried to stay on his feet, but a punch caught the kid in the jaw and sent him spinning to the ground in a dusty cloud. The others beat him for a while and then stopped. He rolled on the ground for a few minutes and slowly stood up. The crowd hooted, and a group of guys led the beaten kid to a chair so he could sit. Then they gave him a beer.

"It's your turn, Martin. Come on, homes. I know you're not scared. They're all waiting."

What was I gonna do? I'd known Frankie for years, and right now he was the closest thing to a brother I had left. And here he was talking about family.

Next thing I know, I'm standing in the circle, and guys start pounding on me. You know on cartoons how they show stars over your head when you get hit? I never used to believe that, but it's true. You take a shot in the head hard enough, and you'll start to see things.

They roughed me up bad, mostly hitting me in the body. I ain't gonna lie to you. It hurt, but nothing like the hurt inside. The pain I felt when Huero died was worse than anything this crew could dish out.

One kid hit me in the jaw, and I snapped and went after him. I was saying something, but I don't know what it was. I just charged like he was the kid who shot Huero. Maybe for a second I thought he was. I can't remember. But I do remember what Oscar was saying.

"Check out Martin! He's lost it. He's *loco*!"

I was so mad, I couldn't control the punches I threw. I didn't care anymore about what happened. Each time I swung, the other guys just hit me harder. They clocked me solid a few times, and I started growling like this angry dog Huero found one day. It had rabies, and white foam was dripping from its mouth before the animal control people killed it. When Frankie finally pulled me away, I was a mess. Bloody spit on my chin, dirt in my hair. My shirt ripped, bruises everywhere. Bruises on top of bruises.

Three pretty girls watching shook their heads and laughed at me like I was a joke or something. I saw one boy spit out his beer because he was nearly choking, unable to stop himself from cracking up. It was like I was the entertainment, a freak show to amuse them. It just made me angrier seeing their smiles while I was hurting inside for Huero.

"*Whatcha lookin' at?*" I hissed.

"Calm down, homes. You're one of us, Martin. We always got your back now," Frankie said when he pulled me out of the circle. He almost seemed proud, like I was some kind of trophy for him. Some guys cheered when Frankie took me away. Someone even poured beer on me.

"Chill, dude," the kid said. The beer

stung the cuts on my face. I should have pounded him.

Frankie dropped me home after midnight. But Mom was awake when I got there. Her face turned white when she saw me, like she was about to throw up.

"*Mijo!*" she cried hesitantly, throwing her arms around me. "What happened to you?"

"Nothin', Ma. I'm fine." I said, shrugging her off and heading to my bedroom. Just looking at her made me feel guilty.

The next morning, a police officer, Nelson Ramirez, came over to our house. He was a friend of my mother's who patrolled outside the Wal-Mart where she worked. He and my mom had dated for a while, but now they are just friends. My mom always seemed to have him over when she thought I needed one of those "man-to-man talks." Like I'm supposed to let this man be my dad or something just 'cause he has a badge. Every time he visited, I had to roll my eyes 'cause he always acted like he knew everything. He's one of those people who tells you what you think.

"You okay, Martin?" he asked. "Imelda . . . I mean, your mother says you might have something you want to tell me about."

"I don't have nothin' to say to you," I told him. The cops were supposed to be investigating Huero's case. But I wasn't holding my breath for that. Kids are shot every day in the barrio, and I don't see police, like in the movies, always getting the bad guy. Especially not for people like me who don't live in the suburbs and drive nice cars.

"Those boys you hang with are gonna pull you down, Martin. Especially Frankie. He may act like your friend, but he's no good."

"Why don't you worry about the dude who shot my brother and leave my friends alone," I snapped back. "They ain't the problem."

He shook his head, sighed, and walked away. Then I heard him talking to my mom in the living room. Little did I know how much their conversation would change my life.

"I can't lose him, Nelson," I heard her say. "It would kill me. He's everything to me."

I should have gone out and told her what she wanted to hear. "You're not going to lose me, Ma." But I couldn't bring myself to it. I felt guilty, but I didn't care. It was like I was dead inside, like my heart had turned gray and rotten once Huero passed away.

All I wanted was the blood of the person who shot my brother.

Nothing else.

"We're moving, *mijo*," my mother said a week later. I was about to leave with the whole posse when she told me. "I'm getting you out of here before I lose you." She was drying dishes in the kitchen sink, and I was standing at the edge of the doorway.

"What?"

"I know what you do. You, Frankie, and the whole bunch of you are looking for the person who shot Huero. If you find him, you're gonna throw your life away or get killed. I can't let you do it."

"I ain't movin'," I said. "I'm staying right here."

The glass in her hand dropped into the sink and shattered, but she didn't seem to notice. Her eyes were wild and stormy-looking.

"No! You are coming with me, so I can save you, *mijo*. Mr. Ramirez helped me find another apartment that I can afford. You'll be going to Bluford High

School. It's safer, and you'll be away from Frankie and all *this*." She waved her hand in a circle as if our whole world was poisoned.

"*Bluford*?" I had heard of the school only a few times. I knew it was in a different section of the city, one with more blacks. My school was mostly Chicanos with some blacks, and a few whites. "I ain't goin' there," I said.

"You *will* go there!" she screamed, coming at me as if she wanted to hit me. "You will or you'll kill me, *mijo*. Do you understand?! You're my only son. My last baby. You're all I have in this world, and this world is trying to take you from me. I see it in your eyes," she said, putting her hands to my face. Her touch almost burned me inside. I could see her tears again too. For a second, I felt my eyes sting, but then I shook it away.

Outside, I heard the rumble of Frankie's car. For once, he had good timing. I had to get away from my mother. She made me hurt. "I gotta go," I said, and I walked out.

"*Martin*!" she yelled, but I closed the door.

I could still hear her voice when I got to Frankie's car. She screamed the same way she did when she learned that Huero was dead. It was like I was gone already, the walking dead.

"What's your problem, homes? You're all quiet," Frankie asked me when I sat in the passenger seat.

I told Frankie and the boys my mom's plan.

"*Bluford*?" Chago said. "Man, what's your mom gonna do that for? I don't know anybody who goes to that school. It's like another country from what I hear."

"My friend had a cousin who went there," Jesus said. "She went off to college a few years ago."

"*College*," Junie said. "Ain't no one from my family gone to college."

Everyone was quiet. We all knew that Junie's dad worked as a TV repairman, and his mom was a house cleaner. It was no big deal. All of our parents had jobs like that. My mom was a cashier.

"Why she want you to go to Bluford?" Chago asked.

"She says she wants to save me," I said.

"How's taking you away from your family gonna save you?" Frankie said, taking a puff of his cigarette.

I looked at him, and he hit the accelerator. The Le Mans grumbled and lurched forward, and I opened the window to get rid of Frankie's smoke and clear my own head.

My family. I didn't even know what that was anymore.

That same night, we hit another party, and I got into a fight with some kid for bumping into me. I know I shouldn't have done it. The kid bumped into me by accident as he turned a corner. Some of his drink, a cherry soda, spilled on my shirt. I moved right into his face. I was just looking for an excuse to start trouble. That's exactly what he gave me.

"Sorry, man," the kid said. He looked nervous. I could see it in his eyes and in the slight waver of his voice, like ripples in a puddle when you hit it with a rock.

"You better watch where you're walking or you could get hurt, homes," I said, giving him a shove.

He said something, and the next thing I knew I threw him against the wall and hit him. I felt bad even as I did it. He couldn't handle me. He was weaker and slower. Unprepared.

My fists slammed into his soft

stomach full force. As I hit him, I could feel my eyes burning again, like there was smoke in them. But no one near me was smoking this time. Instead, my homeboys were standing around me, staring at me like I had horns sprouting from the side of my head. Like I had a disease they were afraid to catch.

The kid put his hands up to defend himself, even as he went down. I even made him flinch once by pretending to swing again. I was ugly and mean, but it felt good to strike back at someone. At anyone. Even this poor dumb kid who didn't know me and who I didn't know. Another kid who should have been home safe with his family, not lying in the dirt.

"He's done, Martin. Come on. Let's go," Frankie said, pulling me back. I stood my ground for a minute longer, hoping the kid would try to get up. But he had more sense than that.

You are coming with me, so I can save you, mijo.

My mom's words kept echoing in my head like one of those songs on the radio that you hate but you just can't stop hearing in your mind.

I looked at the kid. He was cowering

and scared. He had no idea what happened or why.

"Can she save this?" I said, turning with my hands outstretched to my homeboys, my new brothers. Sorry replacements for the one I loved most and lost. Again the acid sting in the eyes.

Frankie looked at me warily. "Let's go, homes."

I spat in front of the kid and left, wondering what his mom would say when he finally got home.

Later that night, I crashed at Frankie's sister Nilsa's crib. She was in her twenties, had a son, and knew not to ask me or Frankie what we did that night. I knew I wouldn't sleep much but at least I didn't have to go home to my mom.

Still, I couldn't get comfortable on Nilsa's couch. A broken spring kept stabbing me, and there were sharp toys wedged between the cushions.

At one point, I turned over and felt something hard poking me in the back of the head. I reached over and pulled out a toy gun. I was the only one in the room, which was black except for the digits on Nilsa's VCR clock, but I started laughing out loud.

The fake gun just set me off. The way it hit me in the head right where Huero was shot. I know it was just a toy, but it's messed up when toys look exactly like the thing that took out your brother. The world is falling apart when that happens. I ain't preaching. I played with toy guns too. So did Huero. But you gotta admit, it's messed up.

It was about 4:00 in the morning, and I was just lying on the couch thinking about all this and laughing. Not 'cause it was funny. But because, what else can you do? I ain't like my mom. I'm not gonna cry. Huero's still gone. All the tears in the world weren't going to change that. Only me and my boys could do something that mattered.

But I knew, not far away, my mom was home worrying about me. I could feel it. She was probably kneeling in front of the picture of Huero praying that I would come home safe. In my mind, I could see her face in the red glow of the prayer candles she got from our church, tears rolling down her cheeks, a crumpled tissue in her hand.

I could have called her to let her know I was all right. Frankie had a cell phone he said I could use. But I didn't.

Instead, I let her worry all night long. I was showing her that she wasn't going to control me. Especially not while me and my boys still had to settle the score for Huero.

But when I got home the next day, my mom had a surprise for me.

It was just after 11:00 a.m. on a Sunday when Frankie dropped me off. I timed it so my mother would still be in church. At least then I wouldn't have to deal with her as soon as I walked in the door. But I was wrong.

She was standing in the living room as soon as I entered. Her eyes were swollen and bloodshot, like she hadn't slept in a week. Her hair was messy, and she looked exhausted.

"Let's go," she said.

Behind her, I noticed that our small apartment was completely empty. Our old sofa, end tables, and TV were gone. All the family pictures on the wall were missing. Even our small kitchen, which I could see from the front door, was bare. The cheap metal cabinets were open and empty. The air smelled of lemons and bleach, the way it did whenever my mother cleaned.

"Let's go, *mijo*," she said, her voice heavy and serious.

"Where's all our stuff, Ma?"

"It's at our new place. I told you we were moving, and that's what we're doing. Now. Come on," she said, trying to lead me toward the door.

"I ain't goin' nowhere, Ma," I said, refusing to budge.

"This isn't your decision, Martin. You're only sixteen years old. I'm still your mother, and you're coming with me. Let's go!" she ordered.

I stepped back. She'd hadn't spoken to me like this since I was a little kid. I wasn't sure how to respond. I walked to my room so I could get away from her and nearly fell over. All my stuff was missing. My bed. My pictures. My whole room. Gone. There were even those marks on the carpet where it had been vacuumed. She cleared me out.

Huero's room was empty and clean too. Like he never lived there. How could she?

"Where's our stuff?!" I yelled, my temper beginning to swell like your eye after someone punches you. "What did you do, Ma?"

"We got a new apartment, Martin. I started packing last night when you took off. I called some people from church and they helped me. Everything's at our new home. Come on," she said.

"I ain't going nowhere. This is my home, and this is where I'm staying!" I said, stepping right into her face like she was just another kid on the street looking for trouble. I was taller than her, and I could feel the veins in my neck pounding. I felt strong with anger, like it was alcohol in my blood.

But she came right back at me, her voice growing louder, making her seem larger than ever.

"No, *mijo*! This is *my* house! I pay the rent. I pay the bills. And you are my son. I'm taking you, and we are leaving right now. End of story." Again she yanked on my arm to take me out.

I twisted away from her and raised my hand. I was about to pop like a fat blister.

She flinched for an instant, bracing for a slap from me. But she did not back down.

"You gonna hit your own mother now?" she said, a flash of fear in her eyes. "Did I lose you already?"

I blinked, lowered my hand, and turned away.

It was like she'd just sent a knife to my heart, like she'd cut my legs off with a machete. There I was, making my mom cringe in fear. There I was, her pride and joy, making her scared the way my Dad used to. I was becoming a monster.

"I don't know what's wrong with me, Ma," I said, unable to look at her. I leaned against the wall at the edge of Huero's room and started butting my head against the plaster. Somehow, the pain felt good, something that made sense.

"Come with me, *mijo*," she said. "Let's get out of here."

Like she did when I was a little kid in a crowded parking lot, my mom led me to her car.

I sat next to her, my head in my hands, as she said a silent prayer, crossed herself, and left our neighborhood for good.

Chapter 3 ·

"Just chill for a while, homes. You started losing it the other night. I heard you laughing in your sleep. That's messed up," Frankie said.

You know it's bad when a guy with a knife-wound in his stomach and a gun in his car tells you to relax.

"I hate this. It's like I'm in prison or something," I said. I was standing at a pay phone down the street from our new apartment. My mom had refused to set up a phone in our place because she wanted to cut me off from my friends. She used a cell phone for all her calls. I was allowed to use it but only in front of her.

"It's for your own good. You need to make new friends. The ones you have are only going to lead you to trouble," Mom had said when she made her decision.

She made me feel like I was three years old. It didn't matter, though. She couldn't stop me from grabbing some change and using a pay phone.

"Martin, I'm gonna find the person who shot Huero," Frankie assured me. "When I do, we'll come for you. Right now, you're too far away to do anything, so just chill."

I hated that Frankie was right. My mother moved us to the other side of the city. To get back home, I had to take a fifty-minute stop-and-go trip by bus, one I'd have to pay for. There was no getting around it; I was stuck.

I hung up the phone and started walking. Anything to pass the time. You can only watch so much TV in the middle of the day before you start to really go crazy.

The new neighborhood was completely different from back home. For one thing, there were black people everywhere, old and young, on the street. Where I came from, almost everyone was Chicano or Mexican. We had blacks in a few houses, but we didn't really hang out with them, and they didn't hang with us. That was just the rule, and no one said anything.

It's the same with the white people. They didn't live anywhere near us, and they always seemed scared when they made a wrong turn and ended up on my street. But they weren't scared when they were looking for a Mexican housekeeper or someone to take care of their yard, pick their vegetables. To them, we were all the same, even though my mom was a third generation American. She hardly ever speaks Spanish. I don't even know it, except for a few words.

Some day, if I ever get a house with a yard, I want to hire white people to cut my grass. Just because.

Besides blacks, I saw a little shop owned by what I guessed were Chinese people. Then there was a pizza shop called Niko's. Those people were white, but they weren't speaking a language I knew.

Down the busiest street near my place, I found a restaurant that looked kind of nice called the Golden Grill. All the cars parked in the lot were nice and new. No lowriders with chrome rims and booming systems. I wasn't impressed.

Not far from the Golden Grill was an ice cream stand called Scoops. A pretty white girl with blond hair was working in there. I nodded at her as she cleaned the front window, but she ignored me. It's all good, though. Blond girls aren't my type.

I turned up another street, and quickly the vibe of the neighborhood changed. The houses were squeezed closer together, and broke-down cars lined the street. Some of the homes had iron bars on the windows and doors. Others were rundown and in need of paint. A stop sign on the corner had been spray painted with a tag I didn't recognize. The word "Stop" had been covered in silver paint, and beneath it someone had written the word "Go".

Two black kids in baggy jeans checked me out as I walked.

"Wassup," one boy said. He was standing on the corner, wearing a black warm-up jacket. The hood was pulled up loosely over his head, though it was warm out. He looked to be my age.

"'Sup," I said. I had lived in the city long enough to know you didn't move through other people's blocks unless you knew where you were going and what you were doing. And if you didn't know those things, you acted like you did. So I moved to the next corner like it was the place I wanted to go. Then I turned back to the main street. I ain't saying I was scared. I'm just not stupid, and these streets were new to me.

I went back toward the pizza place and asked an old woman how to get to Bluford High School. She had a bag full of groceries, and she gave me this you-look-dangerous face.

Please! I thought. *I ain't about to hurt an old woman.*

I couldn't get mad at her, though. Me and my boys got that look whenever we went anywhere as a group. One time Frankie asked a guy on a street corner the time, and the man looked at us and said, "I don't have any money." Like Frankie was gonna steal his wallet or something! Still, when people start treating you like you're a criminal, you start believing you are one. If that guy had given Frankie some money, I bet he would have kept it. I know he would.

Back in the day, I took a kid's bike once when I found it lying unprotected outside. And one time, Chago and I stole the stereo out of a car that had been left unlocked. But that was two years ago, long before Huero got shot. I was a different person then. Even though we did those things, none of us would just go up and rob a person. Especially not an old lady. That's just low.

I smiled at the woman so she'd know I wasn't there to hurt her. My smile these days is weak, but it worked. After a ten-minute walk following her directions, I was standing in front of my new prison away from home, Bluford High School.

The school was just past a grocery market. On the one side of the lot were some houses and a small park. On the other side, sitting in a ring of protective fence, was Bluford. Made of brick and cement, it looked like a giant fortress.

You could fit two Zamora High schools inside Bluford. It was that big. Behind the school was an outdoor track which circled a full-sized football field. Grey metal bleachers were on either side, and I could see a huge sign in blue and yellow letters: *Home of the Bluford Buccaneers*.

The sign made my stomach feel queasy, the way it gets when you eat too much fast food. I knew the school year was about to begin. I'd heard the dumb back-to-school commercials on the radio, but seeing the sign over the football field made it more real.

I'm not going to lie to you. I hate school. It started in fourth grade when my teacher, Ms. Simon, failed me.

"Martin has attention and behavioral problems," she said with a voice that came more through her nose than her mouth.

What Ms. Simon didn't know was that was just before my dad left, when he was drinking and hitting my mom. Ma would never admit something like that to anyone, especially my teacher, so I just had to repeat my grade. After that, people started treating me like I was stupid, and I stopped taking school seriously. My mom, and even my dad for a time, were always strict about me trying my best, but I gave that up long ago. Instead, I just coasted, hung out, got by, and waited for summer. But with Huero's death, school seemed pointless. A bad joke.

I was thinking all this when a security guard approached me from inside the fence.

"You late for practice, young man?" the guard yelled to me. "You can still get in if you go around front."

Behind him, I could see a few students stepping out onto the football field.

"Na, I'm cool," I said, turning away,

trying not to laugh in the guard's face. I had no time for high school football, coaches, players, the whole bit. That's just not me.

And neither was Bluford.

The morning of my first day at Bluford High School, my mom looked at me with her eyes glowing and hopeful. Like it was my first day of kindergarten, not tenth grade. It took all my strength not to get on a bus home.

"You're going to start fresh here, *mijo*. No more gangs."

"Yes, Ma."

"Try to make me and Huero proud," she said, giving me a kiss. Her eyes were dripping again. I knew the tears were for Huero, not me.

"I will, Ma," I said, turning away from her and thinking ahead to the day me and Frankie would catch that shooter.

"And try to start coming to church again. It's been too long since you were there, *mijo*."

"Okay, Ma."

Good thing she couldn't hear my eyes rolling in my head.

Bluford was a maze of hallways with

freshmen running back and forth like cats in an alley. I was new too, but I wasn't about to run around like that. Instead, I just acted like I was with my homeboys, taking my time to get to where I was supposed to be.

I wore the saggiest jeans I had, a white T-shirt, and white high tops. I put the gold cross around my neck under my shirt, and I cut my hair short, Caesar-style. My look always blended right in at Zamora. At Bluford, I was sure I'd stand out, but I didn't care. I was too cool to rush, too angry to worry. I didn't want to be there, and I wanted the whole world to know it.

I arrived late to my classes. It was the first day, so my first two teachers didn't seem to mind. But then I went to my third period class, English.

"You are all sophomores now, so I expect you to be on time every day," the teacher said, as I walked in five minutes late. The teacher, a light-skinned black man in a shirt the color of Frankie's car, had his back to me.

I stopped and shrugged, looking for a desk. My timing was perfect.

A couple students chuckled, and a pretty girl with wavy black hair flashed me a great smile. I scratched my chin, trying to look cool.

"Excuse me, Mr. Mitchell, sir, but you have a guest," said a guy in the third row. He had a muscular build and a wide grin on his face. I could tell right away that I didn't like him.

"Thank you, Steve," Mr. Mitchell said, turning to me. "Can I help you?"

"Yeah, I think I belong in this class," I said. Twenty-five sets of eyes scanned me like I was for sale. I met their eyes until some of them looked away.

"Are you Martin Luna?" he said, checking a list on his desk. "A transfer student from Zamora High School?"

"Yeah." Some students giggled at the name of my high school.

"Good. You're in the right place. Now, Martin. You're late," he said with a weird smile. I wasn't sure if he was mad or not, and I was distracted by his tie. It was bright red and had a picture of a cartoon character. Tweety Bird, I think.

"I had locker trouble," I said quickly, an excuse that always works in the beginning of the school year.

Mr. Mitchell nodded for a second as if he was thinking about what I said. Yet he was looking at me the whole time, like his eyes were magnifying glasses. "Well, just don't have locker trouble tomorrow. Go ahead and grab a seat."

I heard a few whispers as I made my way to the back row on the left side of the room. I liked sitting in the back where I could see the entire classroom. Plus, it's the best place to be when you don't do your homework.

The girl with the dark hair was only one row in front and over from me. From my seat, I could see her long hair stretching all the way to the middle of her back.

"Well, Martin, welcome to our class and to Bluford High. I'm Mr. Mitchell, and as I just said to your classmates, I expect you to show up on time unless there is a serious reason for you not to be here. Got it?" he said.

I nodded, scratching my chin.

"Is sleep a serious reason, 'cause I'm tired this early in the morning," said a kid in the back row on the opposite side of the room. I could tell he was trying to be funny, but I thought his joke was weak, even though several students chuckled.

"Roylin, that's 'cause you spent all summer messing up on the football field," said Steve, laughing at his own joke.

"Shut up, Morris," Roylin said, looking annoyed.

"Unless you two want to continue this discussion after school this week, I suggest you both pay attention," Mr. Mitchell said. "We've got lots of work to do."

"Absolutely, Mr. Mitchell," Steve said, a smile on his face stretching from ear to ear. He was the kind of kid who always had the last word, the kind of kid I couldn't stand.

I leaned back in my chair and zoned out. I saw Mr. Mitchell pass back some papers and watched as kids started reading, but my mind drifted to Huero and then to my homeboys. I wondered how Frankie and the boys were doing back home. I imagined Huero on his first day of kindergarten several years ago. He was so scared, my mom had to walk him onto the bus. After a few days, school became his favorite place.

"What do you think, Martin?" I heard Mr. Mitchell say, his voice snapped me out of my daydream.

"Huh?" I had no clue what was going on. Somewhere thirty minutes had disappeared.

"Wake up, dude," Steve said.

"Based on the story we just read, and

what you've seen in your life, what do you think makes a person a hero?" Mr. Mitchell asked. I could tell from his voice that he was repeating the question. I could also see that he knew I hadn't been paying attention.

I tried to think quickly. I had no idea what the story was about, and the question annoyed me. "I don't know any heroes." I said. "And if I did, I wouldn't trust 'em."

Mr. Mitchell nodded. "Anybody want to help Martin?"

"A hero is strong and tough," Steve said. "Someone who doesn't back down."

"Good, Steve, but are all strong people heroes?" Mr. Mitchell challenged, even as he wrote Steve's words on the chalkboard.

Then the long-haired girl with the great smile raised her hand. "I think a hero is someone who does the right thing, even if it means she might get in trouble. Like someone who stands up for people who aren't strong like Steve."

Some students laughed. I liked her answer.

"Very nice, Vicky," Mr. Mitchell said, jotting her answer under Steve's. "So are you saying a hero is someone who must take an action?" he asked, his eyes twinkling. "Can you give me an example?"

Just then, the bell rang.

"Saved by the bell," Mr. Mitchell said. "We'll talk more about this tomorrow. Your assignment tonight is to write a paragraph about a person who is a hero to you. Try to give details about this person so readers will understand. It's not going to be graded yet, so don't worry. Just write."

I couldn't believe it. Homework. At Zamora, I skipped it about half the time, but I could see that Mr. Mitchell wouldn't let me get away with that.

"Remember, Martin. Be on time tomorrow," he said as I walked out.

I bit my tongue. Me and that teacher were definitely going to have problems. I knew it.

Vicky was in front of me as I headed into the crowded hallway. She was talking to another girl from our class.

"Teresa, why did I ever go out with Steve?" Vicky said. "He's such a jerk."

"He's not *that* bad," Teresa said.

I laughed quietly as I passed Vicky. At least there was one thing about Bluford that I liked.

Chapter 4

The rest of my first day at Bluford dragged like Frankie's first car, an old Chevette with a half-blown engine. U.S. history with Mrs. Eckerly was boring, though I met a funny kid named Cooper. Algebra II with Mr. Singh was even worse. By the time I got to biology with Mrs. Reed, I was ready to go home.

After study hall where I listened to a snobby girl named Brisana gossip about a weekend party, I went to my last class, Phys. Ed. with Mr. Dooling. I was tired when I finally found the gym. But as soon as I entered the locker room, I spotted Steve Morris. He was giving a high-five to a kid next to him. With his shirt off, I could see he had an athlete's body. Much bigger than me or any of my boys.

"Can you believe that, Clarence?" he said. "One day soon I'm gonna pop Roylin."

"Man, you'd kill him," Clarence said.

"Yeah, but until football season ends, I gotta stay out of trouble. Coach would kick me off the team." I noticed everyone in that section of the locker room was quiet, as if Steve was someone special.

Inside the gym, Mr. Dooling, an older man who looked as tired as me, took attendance and assigned our class to break into groups to play basketball. I admit it. Basketball isn't my sport, and I ain't no LeBron James. So I hung on the sidelines with a couple other kids and watched Steve strut out onto the court.

"Who wants to play me?" he challenged, bouncing a ball hard against the gym floor.

Once the game started, he was an animal on the court, stealing the ball and blocking shots. None of the other guys could touch him. I watched one kid, smaller and quicker than the others, try to defend the basket. The kid's arms were out, his feet were planted, but Steve just charged through him as if he wasn't there. Up went Steve's lay-up while the other guy went smashing to the ground like he'd been hit by a train.

"That's what I'm talking about," Steve boasted, punching his chest. Clarence slapped Steve's hand in triumph.

The other kid lay on the wooden floor holding his head for several seconds before he slowly got up, his feet unsteady. The whole scene just rubbed me the wrong way.

"Easy, Morris. This isn't football," Mr. Dooling warned.

"If it was, he wouldn't be getting up," Steve bragged.

Back in the locker room, Steve kept talking about his basketball game.

"Man, did you see that kid fly? That felt good," he said.

"Steve, you crushed him. He's gonna think twice next time he steps on the court with you," Clarence said. He seemed to follow Steve like a dog looking for scraps.

I tried to ignore them as I waited in line to leave, but then Steve described how he hit the kid. "I was like *WHAP*," he said performing his hit and then laughing about it. Clarence chuckled with him.

Maybe it was because I was tired.

Maybe it was because I hated Bluford, or maybe it was because I missed Huero, and something about seeing that kid on the ground bothered me. I'm not sure. All I know is that I suddenly couldn't take listening to Steve.

"Man, how many times you gonna keep telling us what you did?" I said. "It don't take that much skill to hit someone who's half your size."

A couple kids standing next to me moved away, and Clarence looked a little stunned, as if he'd never heard someone speak the truth to him before.

"Do I know you?" Steve asked, sizing me up.

"You do now," I said.

"You're that loser from Zamora who's in my English class, aren't you?"

"Nah, you're that punk from Bluford in *my* English class," I said, taking a step forward.

Steve's eyes narrowed.

I dropped my books. I wanted my hands free, just in case.

Was I dangerous? Was I a gang-banger? That's what he was thinking. Though he didn't say it, I could see it in his face. He wasn't sure about me.

The bell signaling the end of the day

sounded, and kids started rushing out.

"Come on, Steve. We gotta go to practice," Clarence said.

"You and me are gonna continue this later, Sanchez," Steve said.

"I hope so," I said, eyeing him until he turned the corner.

"That was cool," said a short kid behind me in the locker room. I almost laughed.

Frankie and the boys would be proud.

"How was your day, *mijo*?" my mother asked when she got home. She looked tired. I knew the move increased her own commute to work. She was home an hour later than usual.

"It was fine, Ma," I said, flipping channels on the TV.

"Did you meet anyone new? Tell me about your classes."

"What do you want me to say?" I just wasn't in the mood.

"Martin!"

"Do you want the truth, Ma? Here goes. I didn't feel like talking to anyone. I came late to every class, and I almost started a fight with some big dude. That was my day."

"Don't do this to me," she said, slumping into a living room chair.

I couldn't help it. If you ask me when I am calm, I can say I never want to hurt my mother. But since Huero died, there was almost no calm.

"*You* did this to me, Ma! Now you're acting like everything is supposed to be perfect. Well, it's *not* perfect." I snapped.

She took a deep breath and looked up like she was saying a prayer.

"Martin, I did this for *you.*"

"Well, it's not what I wanted!" My temper was boiling.

"All right, then, what *do* you want?" she challenged, standing up in front of me. "Martin Luna? Who is he? Oh, I know, I think I have it. The neighborhood punk down at the end of the street? No, no! The teenager who wants to miss class all day? Or I got it. The fool who wants to paint a red target on his chest that says to the world, 'Here, come get me!' Is that it, Martin? Did I get it right now?"

I cut the TV off and threw the remote control into the wall. I wanted to punch something.

"I'm sorry this is hard on you, Martin, but if I had done this sooner, maybe Huero wouldn't have been out on the street looking for you," she said, wiping her eyes. "I won't lose another son."

My mind caught on her words, like a shirt snagged on a nail.

Maybe Huero wouldn't have been out on the street looking for you.

She was hinting at something I never allowed myself to say, something I knew haunted my nightmares, fueled my anger, and scared me more than dying itself.

"You think it was my fault, don't you," I said. The room was so quiet that even the silence seemed loud. My mother's eyes widened. The moment is an invisible gash that will never heal.

"Don't do this, Martin."

"Tell me the truth, Ma. You think it's my fault. You're trying to punish me."

"*Martin!*" she said, putting her hand on my shoulder.

I pushed her aside and stormed out of the house.

"Where are you going?" she called, but I ignored her.

I had to get out. Away from her eyes that told me I was guilty. Away from everyone that could see me and know what I had done.

But no matter where I walked that night, no place on earth was dark enough for me, the big brother who failed.

I felt like a ghost the next day as I walked to school. Though I crept back in around 3:00 a.m., I didn't sleep at all, and when I got to Mr. Mitchell's class, I was late again. I hadn't done my homework either.

I opened the door quietly and moved quickly to my chair in the back. I saw Steve, but I couldn't be bothered with him.

"Mr. Luna." I heard Mr. Mitchell's voice as I sat down. I recognized his tone. It was the one that meant you were in trouble.

"Yeah," I said. "Let me guess. I'm busted 'cause I'm late, right?" I wasn't going to play around; I knew what was coming.

"Is there a reason you're late?" he asked, ignoring my comment.

Steve turned in his seat and stared at me. He had that satisfied grin on his face that told me he was enjoying me getting into trouble. Vicky looked back at me too, but then she turned away.

"No. I'm just late again," I said. Several students looked puzzled, as if what I said was not in English.

"I see," said Mr. Mitchell quickly. "Let's discuss this after school. I've got an appointment today, so it'll have to be tomorrow at 3:00. I'll be looking for you."

"What for?" I challenged, standing up at my desk. I knew I should calm down, but I couldn't.

The class got quiet, and I could feel everyone's eyes crawling across me in my black shirt and jeans.

"You're sure his name ain't Martin Looney? He's psycho," Steve mumbled.

"Sit down, Martin. We can talk about this after class," Mr. Mitchell said.

I wanted to throw my desk and hit Steve with my chair. I could almost see the look on his face as the chair crashed down on him. And yet, I knew Steve hadn't done anything serious to me. Just words. That ain't nothing. I was losing it. I don't know how long I stood there, maybe five or ten seconds, before I sat back down in my seat.

Mr. Mitchell seemed relieved and instantly began his lesson. I wiped the sweat from my forehead, picked up my notebook and a pen and started acting like I was a student.

But I only wrote one word in my notebook: H U E R O.

Beneath the word, I drew eyes, my brother's gentle bright eyes. The ones that I see every night staring at me from that bike.

After class, Mr. Mitchell called me to his desk.

"Are you okay, Martin?" he asked. He gave me this look like he was serious, but I wasn't about to share my business with him.

"I'm fine," I said. "Just got a lot on my mind, that's all."

"I know it's not easy switching schools. How are you doing with everything here at Bluford?"

I felt like I was on one of those dumb news shows where the reporter walks up to someone whose house just burned down and says, 'So how do you feel now that you have no place to live?' I had to get away from this guy and his purple tie. This time with Bugs Bunny.

"School's just perfect, Mr. Mitchell. Everything's fine. I wouldn't change a thing." I said it as sarcastically as possible, hoping he would take the hint and let me go. "I'm gonna be late for my next class," I reminded him.

"Okay, Martin, I get it. But let me just say this. If you ever want to talk, or if there is something going on at home or in school that is affecting you, let me know. I've seen a few things in my time, and I may be able to help."

"Whatever you say, Mr. Mitchell," I said, giving him my fake smile.

"Good. So I'll see you on time for class tomorrow and then after school at 3:00, right?" He smiled this time. I nodded just to get him off my back.

"And don't forget to bring your assignment to class too," he said.

I left the classroom as soon as I could. The man made me feel like I was under a spotlight, and after everything that happened, all I wanted was to be in the shadows. I hung low the rest of the day, taking a few notes, blending into the back of the room, trying my best to pretend that the conversation with my mother never happened.

At gym class, I ran into Steve again. He was heading out of the locker room when I was going in.

"Hey, Looney," he said. "That was quite a show you put on in Mr. Mitchell's class. You gonna do that little stand-up thing in here too?" Before I could answer, he was gone.

I slammed my books in the gym locker. I didn't want to lose it again.

"That guy is the biggest jerk," said a voice from behind me. It was the same kid who Steve knocked down the day before.

"You got that right," I said. "I don't know how much more of that I can take."

"He's been that way since middle school, but he's gotten worse now that he's the starting running back for the football team. We both live on the same block, but everyone treats him like he's God or something."

"I don't care who he is. If he keeps acting like that, he's gonna get a surprise from me."

"Don't mess with him. The football team's kinda like a gang around here."

I almost laughed at the word. *Gang.* This boy didn't know the meaning of the word.

"What's your name?" the kid asked.

"Martin. Martin Luna."

"Wassup, Martin. I'm Eric," he said, shaking my hand. "Eric Suarez."

I nearly fell over. The only other Eric

I knew was my brother.

"You all right?" Eric asked.

"Yeah, I'm cool," I said, pushing the memories back. "Let's get to class."

"Hi, Martin. Did you finish your English assignment yet?"

The question caught me by surprise. It was the end of the day, and I was on the main steps leading out of the school. I turned to see Vicky. She was right behind me, wearing white jeans and a light blue jacket.

Teresa was standing with her. For a split second, she gave me this look. I'd seen it before from snobby girls that looked down at guys like me. I recognized it in her face just as plain as if she wore a shirt that said, "Martin Luna is no good. Stay away from him."

But Vicky looked good. *Real good.* The kind of girl you want to stare at even though you know better.

"No," I said. To be honest, I wasn't sure what to say. The girls I usually hung out with at parties never talked about homework, and most of the girls at Zamora who were serious students didn't pay attention to me or my friends.

"Me neither." Vicky spoke quickly,

like she was nervous. "Everything I write seems cheesy, you know, the whole hero thing. I liked what you said yesterday in class, though. It was . . . real."

Her eyes were so intense. I knew she meant what she said. Just seeing her cleared the fog in my head for the first time that day.

"Okay, Vicky, I have to go. Call me later," Teresa said, giving Vicky the what-are-you-talking-to-*him*-for look.

"See ya, T," Vicky said.

I felt kind of felt dishonest because I hadn't even thought about our English assignment. Yet Vicky made me want to think about it. Isn't that weird? Frankie would have teased me if he knew this. *You're getting soft, homes*, he'd say. Good thing he wasn't there.

"I liked what you said too. I bet Steve didn't like it too much," I said. I wanted to see what she would do if I mentioned his name.

"Oh, don't get me started on Steve. All that boy cares about is himself. It's like everyone else exists just to tell him he's great. When you stop doing that, he gets mad at you."

"Yeah, I seen some of that. He's in my gym class," I said as we passed the parking lot down the street from Bluford.

"Too bad for you," she said with a smile.

"It's all right. He don't impress me. So what if he's an athlete? I know people who would scare him off any football field."

Vicky glanced sideways as if something I said bothered her.

"You all right?" I asked.

"What is the problem with you guys?" she said. I could tell it was one of those questions she didn't expect an answer to. "Everything's always about winning and losing. Sure, it's great to win, but then someone else has to lose, get hurt, or whatever. I'm sick of that."

She began to walk faster. I could see she was annoyed. There was this fire in her eyes. It actually made her look even prettier, though I knew not to say something like that.

"Are you saying I should buy Steve a flower each time he starts showing off?" I said, trying to make a joke.

"No," she grumbled, giving me a playful shove. There was a tiny smile trying to break free on her face, but she was fighting it. "I'll see you tomorrow in class," she said, turning up the next street.

I watched her walk away, her long hair waving back at me with each step she took.

Chapter 5

I don't know heroes. There is no
Superman in my life. I stopped
looking for that when I was a kid.
It was better than being let down
all the time. Almost two months ago,
someone looked to me like I was a
hero. He was Huero, my brother,
and he's gone now.

I scribbled the words in my English
notebook after dinner and then slammed
the book shut. I couldn't believe I was
writing. Who was I kidding? I knew what
I wrote wasn't what Mr. Mitchell wanted.
And I'll be honest with you. I was too
scared to keep going. Just those few
sentences made my hand shake like it
does when I drink too much soda. I
couldn't go any further.

"It does my heart good to see you doing your homework, Martin," my mom said, coming up behind me while I was sitting at the table.

She put her hand on my back like she did when I was little. For a second, I felt like I was eight years old again. I didn't speak, but I didn't push her hand away.

"It's gonna be okay here for us, *mijo*," she said. "I believe that."

I couldn't talk because my words suddenly felt all knotted in my throat. The world seemed so twisted. I could have argued with my mother, but I didn't. I don't know why, but I just let her touch me, never mentioning our last conversation, which still hung in the air like an invisible shadow.

The next day I cut school.

I hadn't exactly planned to do it. I'd even prepared to show Mr. Mitchell my paragraph, just to get him off my back. But when I got dressed and finally left our apartment, I just couldn't get myself to go to the school. The closer I got, the harder each step became. Finally, I just turned around, went home, grabbed a few dollars, and headed to the bus station.

A few minutes later, I was sitting on a bus headed back to my old neighborhood. I figured once I got home I'd find Frankie, and we'd hang out. Just like old times, I told myself. But that was a lie. I knew old times ended when we buried Huero. Truth is I just needed to get away from the new apartment, the homework that made me shake, the teacher who got in my face, the pretty girl who challenged me.

I had to get away from Bluford.

After a thirty-minute ride, the bus was so crowded people had to stand in the aisle. Next to me, an elderly white woman carrying a bouquet of flowers struggled to steady herself. I smiled at her, and she turned away without a word, like she was scared of me.

Her look made me feel so low, you know. In her eyes, I was guilty, and she didn't even know me. I couldn't take it.

"Excuse me," I said to her.

A bump shook the bus and she grabbed the edge of my seat. Her fingers looked like old tree roots that grow on top of the ground. But she didn't acknowledge me.

"Ma'am? Excuse me," I said again.

This time she turned around slowly.

Again, her eyes were nervous.

"Would you like to sit down?" I said. "You can have my seat."

The woman hesitated. I knew it would be safer for her to sit, but I could see she felt the opposite. "Really, it's okay," I assured her. I needed her to believe me, to believe that I could do something good. Not just scare her.

"Why, yes. That would be nice," she said finally, watching me carefully.

I got up and moved out of her way so she could sit. I am sure she was glad to have a busload of people around to watch over her.

Outside, the passing streets began to look familiar. I was getting close to home.

"Thank you," I heard the woman say in a scratchy voice.

"You're welcome, ma'am," I said. I tried to act like it was no big deal. Up ahead, I saw the tall bell tower of our church, St. Ignatius. Huero's grave was just a few blocks away. I hadn't been there since the funeral.

The woman's bundle of flowers rubbed against my arm, and I looked down at them.

"They're for my husband," she said.

"He died three years ago. I was going to visit him last week, but I wasn't up to it. Not always easy getting around when you get to be my age. You'll see," she said with a smile.

"I'm sorry about your husband, ma'am," I said. I could feel that burning in my eyes again. I don't know why it happened on the bus like that. Maybe the flowers were giving me allergies or something, I don't know.

I couldn't imagine living to be an old person. And I could not deal with the idea of being old without my little brother. I still can't. I just had to visit him. As soon as the bus neared the cemetery, I pulled the cord signaling the driver to stop. When the door opened, I climbed down and saw the woman following me. She made her way down the steps slowly, but her face seemed so determined I didn't know whether I should help her. Still, I tried.

"Thank you for being such a gentleman," she said politely. "You don't see that much anymore."

"You're welcome," I said, looking at the sea of headstones stretching back from the road.

There's too many dead people, Huero

66

once said when we walked by the cemetery years ago. The comment seemed so funny at the time that I laughed out loud then. Now it just hurts.

"You don't have to walk me there, son. I can manage it myself," the lady said to me when she reached the street corner outside the gates. I think she still wasn't totally sure about me.

"I'm here to see someone too, ma'am." I explained. "My little brother."

The woman's face softened instantly, like inside some kind of switch had been flipped. Though I can stare down any dude on the street, I couldn't look this old lady in the eye. Not then.

"Oh no," she said, her voice fading off for a second. "No young person should have to go through such pain," she said, putting her shaky veined hand on my arm. A second later, she reached into her flower bundle and pulled out a red rose. "Here, take this," she insisted. "Give it to your brother."

I took the flower, but I couldn't speak to thank her.

Together we made our way into the cemetery. The old woman went one way, and I went the other. We were two people who could not have been more different. But that morning I felt closer to the white-haired woman than anyone else I knew.

Ain't that messed up?

At Huero's headstone, I sat down on the ground and felt the warm earth under my legs. It was peaceful and quiet.

"I miss you, little brother," I said out loud. I then told him what had happened since he died. I described the move and the new high school. I even mentioned Vicky just so Bluford wouldn't sound too depressing.

"Me and Frankie are still tight," I assured him as if it would be important to Huero. All Frankie ever really did was help me chase Huero away.

I swear to this day I still hear the squeak of that bike and see Huero's eyes.

The one thing I could not say to Huero was what Frankie and I were planning. It just didn't feel right imagining Huero knowing about us shooting someone.

Nearby, a young man and his girlfriend were doing the same thing as me, sitting in front of a headstone and talking out loud to someone buried in the ground. Someone they loved who died.

Don't think it's strange. If you haven't suffered through this, you're just lucky. You will lose someone one day. All of us do. When it's your turn, remember me and Huero.

I left the old woman's rose on the edge of Huero's stone and headed over to Frankie's. It was about 11:00 a.m. when I got there.

"Wassup, homes?" he said as soon as he saw me. He was working on his Le Mans, as usual. Some things didn't change. "How's Bluford? Not too good if you're here already," he said, laughing at his comment.

"Bluford stinks, Frankie. I hate it."

"Any cute girls there?" he said. "You gotta hook me up, bro."

"One. But she's not your type," I said. "Too smart for you."

Frankie laughed. I pretended it was like old times for a minute, but I knew it wasn't. The strange silence that filled the air like a cloud of smoke was proof that everything had changed.

"So what's up? How'd you get here?"

"I took a bus. Then I went to visit Huero. My first time since . . . you know."

Frankie lit a cigarette and said nothing. It's what he always did when something bothered him. I turned on the radio in his car, just to cut down the silence.

"We're gonna take them out, Martin. Me and Chago been asking around. I made him and Junie get guns. We getting stronger every day, homes. Tonight, Chago's seein' this girl Lisa who's got people everywhere. I'd bet money she knows something. Trust me. As soon as that car appears, we'll know it."

I felt like I was hearing him from far away. Like he was on a bad phone connection with me or something.

"My mom thinks it was my fault."

"*What?*"

"She said if I hadn't been out on the street, Huero wouldn't have been shot. And you know what, Frankie? She's right, man. No one was after Huero. You know it too. He was just in the wrong place at the wrong time because of me," I said, stomping a beer can into the concrete. "You know what's worse, Frankie? He looked to me to help him. I could see it in his eyes, bro."

"Shut up, homes!" Frankie yelled. "You didn't pull that trigger. It's not like you knew what was happening. You can't be blamin' yourself 'cause you never did nothing to deserve that," he said, taking a long drag from his cigarette and tossing the butt into the street.

"I never said this to you, but I guessed you'd figure it out 'cause you're smart. But that bullet was probably meant for me, homes," Frankie said, looking at me more seriously than ever. "I'm the only one in our crew with a reputation. The rest of you are just little wannabes, except for you, Martin. You might be something one day."

I sat down on the curb. My head felt ready to explode. Frankie's words made too much sense. Whenever all of us went out, it seemed the whole world knew Frankie. It even got to the point where the rest of us were almost jealous of him. At parties, people would say his name as if he was a TV star or something. His knife wound, his mysterious past, his willingness to fight, and his car just added to his reputation. Compared to him, the rest of us were nobodies.

But I never thought about the target of the bullet that killed Huero. Like the newspaper, I just made the story simple. "8-Year Old Gunned Down in Gang-Related Shooting." From the beginning, my response was simple. Just go after the person that hurt my brother. Now, Frankie just made the picture more complicated.

"How long have you thought about all this, Frankie?"

"From the beginning. But it don't matter. You and me are family. Remember? When someone takes out your brother, they're taking out my brother. So we are in this together, homes. Like I said, we'll get them as soon as I find them."

I'm serious when I tell you all this had my head spinning. I felt dizzy. I know Frankie thought his words were supposed to comfort me, but they didn't. Instead, I had that nagging feeling that you get when you know you're forgetting something important, but you don't know what it is.

"You're still down with this, right, homes?" Frankie asked me, studying my face strangely. "You're not getting soft or nothing?"

"No, I'm down, Frankie. Don't worry." But as I said the words, I was thinking that Frankie should have told me people were after him. If he had, I would have found a way to keep Huero away. Maybe

I could have saved him.

"Cool, Martin," Frankie said, getting in his car and starting the engine. "Let's get out of here."

I spent the rest of the day with Frankie. After visiting two auto parts shops, we worked on his car, grabbed some burgers, and picked up the rest of the boys. We hung out in Chago's garage. Junie and Frankie shared a joint. It wasn't the first time. I even drank half a beer, trying to pretend that I was like the rest of the guys, hanging out, telling stories, chilling.

But who was I kidding? The beer tasted nasty, like dog pee. The boys' jokes didn't seem as funny. All the smoke stunk up my clothes. And Frankie kept watching me. He knew I was different, but I doubt if he knew why.

It was about 8:00 when Frankie drove me home. He made me direct him to Bluford first just so he could see my school.

"This ain't your world, homes," he said, studying the school, and then staring at me.

I nodded. He was right, but I wasn't sure what my world was. Not anymore.

"Martin, if there is something you need to tell me, you should do it. It ain't good to keep things hidden from your brother," he said once we got to my mom's apartment.

His words seemed false to me. If he had followed his own advice, maybe Huero would still be alive.

"Don't worry, Frankie. When I have something to say, you'll know it."

Chapter 6

My mother was sitting in the living room with Officer Ramirez when I walked in. I wasn't in the mood to see either one of them.

"Where were you?" Mom asked me as soon as I walked in. She got up and stood in front of me. "You stink. What were you doing?" Her questions came as fast as punches.

I knew what she said was true. I smelled like beer and smoke.

"Nowhere, Mom."

"Don't tell me 'nowhere.' I got a message from your school today. They said you were absent." I could see that Mom was upset, but she was working hard to stay calm, probably because of Officer Ramirez. "Now where were you?"

"Calm down, Ma," I said, ignoring her

question and looking at the cop. "Did you bring him here to yell at me?"

"No, Martin," Officer Ramirez said. "I brought your mother home from work, and I thought I'd just check in with you. From the looks of things, you could use some help."

"I don't need *your* help." All his help ever brought was bad news. *We don't know who the killer was. Maybe you should move to a new neighborhood. Go to a new school.*

"Martin, I'm going to ask you this one more time. Where were you today?"

The room got quiet, and I looked at them both. Even Officer Ramirez looked serious.

"I went to visit Huero, Mom," I admitted. "After that I went to see Frankie. I'll go to school tomorrow," I said before turning to my room.

No one said anything when I shut my bedroom door.

Thursday I made it to English class on time. I'm not saying I did it for my mom or Mr. Mitchell or anyone. I just did it. Don't ask me why.

Mr. Mitchell was standing by the door ready to close it as soon as the bell rang. "We missed you yesterday, Martin. Everything all right?" he asked.

"Yeah, why? You see something wrong?" I said. He looked almost hurt, but I didn't care. He was just too nosy.

"Let's reschedule that detention for this afternoon," he replied as I quickly passed him.

Vicky was at her seat when I went to my desk but was fishing something out of her backpack when I passed her.

"You coming to the big game Saturday, Mr. Mitchell?" Steve asked as he walked in.

"Actually, I'll be here, Steve. I'm handling Saturday detentions. Maybe I'll check out the game," said Mr. Mitchell.

"Zamora's goin' down, Mr. Mitchell. You should come out and see me score," he replied, turning to me.

I made a snorting sound at Steve, just to get on his nerves. I never cared about Zamora's football team, although I have to admit it would be nice to see Zamora win.

Vicky shook her head and wrote something in her notebook. Nearby, I heard Teresa sigh. That girl has no time for me.

Mr. Mitchell started class with a

discussion of an old story called *Beowulf* that the class had started reading the day before. I had no idea what he was talking about. Something about a monster in the woods that had all these people scared until someone was brave enough to stop it. I never heard of the story, but it kind of sounded like my neighborhood.

Always something lurking around, taking out kids.

Toward the end of class, Mitchell brought the discussion back to heroes. "For the last ten minutes of class, I want you to team up with a partner or two and look at the paragraphs you wrote for homework. Follow the steps we discussed yesterday to give helpful suggestions to your partner. Final drafts are due tomorrow."

All around me, students moaned, and I leaned back in my chair. I hate when teachers make you share your work. It's like having people spy on you when you're in the shower. The only good thing was that I sat in the back row. I was sure none of the students there did their work.

I turned to my right and saw that kid Roylin looking at me. He was the only other kid in the back row, and he had this dumb smile on his face that told me he hadn't even opened his book. Good. At least I wasn't the only one.

"Martin, why don't you team up with Vicky and Teresa. Roylin, you work with Steve and Darcy," Mr. Mitchell said. Teresa's face scrunched up like she'd just smelled Frankie's boots. It was almost funny.

"Are you sure I gotta have him in my group?" Steve said about Roylin.

"Well, you could always join me Saturday instead of playing in that big game."

I laughed out loud along with several other students.

"Morris, if your head gets any bigger, it ain't gonna fit in your helmet," Roylin cut back.

"Gentlemen. Enough. You're on the same team. Figure out how to work together. That's more important than football or English," Mr. Mitchell said.

I had to give the teacher some credit. His comment shut them up.

I got out of my desk and sat next to Vicky. She was jotting something into one of those planner notebooks. None of my friends would ever buy such a thing.

Her handwriting was so tiny, I couldn't read it, but I could see that it was perfectly straight and even, unlike mine.

"I can't read that chicken scratch," my English teacher said last year. I got a C– in the class and didn't worry about it. As long as I passed.

Vicky seemed the opposite of the girls who I hung out with back home. Her face was so intense. It was like she had ten things racing through her mind, all of them related to school. Luisa, the last girl I dated, would have laughed at someone like Vicky. Even if Luisa had ten things in her head, school would be number eleven. I'm not dogging her, though, because I was no better.

Teresa slid her desk toward us. It made a loud groaning sound as she nudged it forward a few inches at a time. As she approached, she looked at me like I was a dentist who was about to pull out her tooth. I leaned back and waited.

"Let me just say that what I wrote was bad," Vicky said, grabbing another notebook and flipping to the pages she wanted to show us.

"You always say that, Vic, but you know it's not true," Teresa said.

"I don't think I did the assignment right, and I didn't get to finish," I said. The idea of showing them what I wrote about Huero bothered me.

Teresa stared at Vicky as if I wasn't there. *See, I told you he was stupid,* her look said.

"Let's just exchange and do what Mr. Mitchell said. Just helpful suggestions."

"Whatever," Teresa said.

We switched notebooks. Teresa got mine; Vicky got Teresa's, and I got Vicky's. When she handed it to me, she smiled. Her long hair was pulled back, and she looked so nice I got a little nervous. Don't laugh at me. It's true.

Her paragraph was about her grandmother who came from Mexico without an education. When she arrived in the U.S., she couldn't even read, but she managed to go to night school, graduate from college and become a teacher. In the two-page paper, Vicky said her grandmother inspired her to work hard and value education. Now she's hoping to be a teacher too.

"This is good, Vicky," I said, putting her notebook down. "You should read it to your grandmother. It would make her proud."

"I can't," she said with a look I won't forget. "She died two years ago."

I felt like kicking myself. It wasn't the first time I said something stupid, but it felt like it. "I'm sorry," I said, trying to think of the right words to say. My tongue was suddenly a tangled knot.

"It's okay, Martin," she said, turning to Teresa and offering her a few writing suggestions. My turn was next, and Teresa began by shaking her head and frowning.

"I don't think what you wrote is what Mr. Mitchell wanted. It's not long enough either," she said. "But I guess it's . . . okay." Teresa spoke the last word as if was especially difficult.

"Thanks, Teresa," I said, wanting to tell her off, but Vicky was there. Instead, I gave her a big fake smile. "That's *really* helpful."

"Okay, let's switch again," Vicky instructed. This time I got Teresa's paper, and Vicky got mine.

My stomach was flipping while Vicky was reading my short paragraph about Huero. I was afraid she'd think I was dumb or something, but what could I do? I wasn't a writer. After several long seconds, she brushed her hair back and looked at me.

"I don't know what to say," she said. Teresa yawned.

"I know. I didn't do the assignment right."

"No, Martin. What you wrote is so . . . deep. But I don't understand. You need to finish it. You need to explain what happened to your brother."

"Someone shot and killed him." I spoke the words in the same way I would tell you my favorite color, the day I was born, the name of Frankie's sister. Sitting in front of Teresa and Vicky with the whole class nearby, I wasn't gonna lose it.

"I'm so sorry," she said.

"It's okay, Vicky," I told her. Yet I could feel the movement inside, like the little earthquakes we get around here from time to time. Not enough to hurt anyone. Just enough to let you know something is happening.

She looked at me with those brown eyes, and I could see sadness in them for me. I felt naked like a newborn baby. It might sound silly to say that when you have a pretty girl in front of you. But it wasn't like she was seeing my body without clothes on. It was like she was looking at my insides. Like I had no skin. I almost freaked.

"Your paper was great, Vicky," Teresa said, shattering the moment instantly. I was glad she did. "I wouldn't change a thing.

"Yours was nice too, Teresa. Really *nice*," I said, giving her exactly what she gave to me.

Truth is, I didn't read a word of Teresa's paper. It could have been about the planet Mars for all I cared! My mind was on Vicky.

It took me all day to calm down from English class. I couldn't shake the feeling Vicky gave me. I wanted to talk to her, but I had no idea what I would say. I used to think I was pretty smooth around girls, but not with her.

In gym class, Mr. Dooling continued his unit on basketball, and again I found myself on the court. This time, I had to play a little bit.

"C'mon, Luna, get in the game," Mr. Dooling yelled when he spotted me on the sidelines.

Next thing I knew, I was on the court dribbling the ball.

As soon as I got near our opponent's

basket, I passed the ball to one of my teammates who dribbled three steps, drawing the defenders away from me. Then he passed it right back.

"Shoot it!" he yelled.

I was about as far from the basket as the foul line, but I was off to the side. It looked to be a pretty easy jump shot, even for me. I planted my feet, raised the ball, brought up my arms, and went to shoot.

Just as I was about to let the ball go, I saw a blur through the corner of my eye. A split second later, wind rushed by me the way it does when a car passes you on the street. The ball, which had been on the tips of my fingers, was knocked loose from my hands.

"Rejected!" someone cheered.

"What happened?" I said, turning around.

Behind me, I could see someone zigzagging down the court with the ball. He stopped briefly at midcourt to dribble behind his back and through his legs. Just to show off.

The guy was fast, and he was bigger than most of the kids in the gym. I knew right away who blocked my shot. It was Steve Morris.

"Morris, give back that ball, and get off the court until it's your turn to play," Mr. Dooling yelled.

"He smoked you, man," said a voice on the other side of me. I looked to see Clarence standing there. That stupid smile was on his face.

Many people in the gym who knew Steve were laughing. Other kids, including Eric, were watching me. Many had that hungry look people get when there's going to be a fight. But none of them knew me, so they didn't know how I'd react. If Frankie was there, he could have told them what was going to happen. You probably already know by now.

I started walking down the other end of the court toward Steve. He was still showboating.

"Don't do it, Martin," said Eric from behind me.

There was no stopping me. I had to do something. I just didn't know exactly what.

"Morris, give that ball back," Mr. Dooling said. It sounded to me like he was begging.

"Just one shot, Mr. Dooling," answered Steve.

"Slam it, Steve!" Clarence chanted.

"Dunk it!"

I can't stand that kid.

Steve glanced up at the basket and began to dribble toward it slowly, setting his steps right so he could dunk it. I couldn't let that happen. Not on me.

I picked up my pace toward Steve. His back was still to me while he worked to set up his shot. I knew he had no clue where I was. Suddenly he started jogging to the basket. If I was going to stop him, I'd have to move quick.

I broke into a full sprint. It was a race against time, but I was faster because I didn't have to deal with the ball.

Steve took two big steps, following a curved path that would lead to the right side of the basket. I charged straight in, making my trip shorter. We were like two meteors streaking to the same point.

Just as he took his third step and was about to jump up, I crossed his path. His arms were on their way up, but I came crashing down on the ball, knocking it free from his hands. It bounced hard off his leg and hopped back into the court. I flew out of bounds and nearly smashed into the cinderblock wall of the gym.

"Man, what are you trying to do?" Steve said as I steadied myself.

"*Trying*? Homes, I just *did* it."

I raised my hands over my head and looked back at my class. Instantly, the whole place erupted in hoots. It seemed like everyone, even the other gym teachers, stopped to see what was happening. I would have stopped too. It's not everyday the star running back of the football team gets shown up by a kid like me.

"All right, that's enough, you two," Mr. Dooling said from somewhere behind me.

I walked back to my classmates without another word. I had nothing else to say. But Steve wasn't done.

Chapter 7

"You gonna stand for that, Steve?" Clarence said. I could hear his voice behind me.

"Yo, Steve. I don't know who that kid is, but he just schooled you, man," another kid said.

I picked up the ball and moved back to center court. I wasn't going to back down from Steve, but I wasn't going to get in trouble for him either.

"All right, everyone. Enough. Steve, get off the court," Mr. Dooling said. Steve had this disgusted look on his face, like he had just swallowed a rotten egg.

"Yo, that was awesome, dog," said a kid on my team. Other kids stared at me oddly as if *I* was the one that did something wrong. I just don't understand some people. It don't matter, though. It was the best day I had in school in years.

We played our game until the bell rang. But just as everyone started heading back into the locker room, I heard footsteps coming up behind.

"Look out!" someone yelled.

I braced myself.

Suddenly something exploded against my shoulder, and then I was rolling to the ground, my face smacking off the hard wood of the basketball court. Several people stood around me for a few seconds, blocking the view of teachers. I still remember their shoes. Adidas and a pair of high top Nikes.

And then there was Steve's grinning face.

"Don't mess with me, Martin. I don't lose," he said, and walked away. No teachers were in sight. Everyone was in the locker room.

It took me a while to sit up. When Steve blindsided me, the impact knocked the air from my lungs, and I gasped like a fish out of water for several seconds. At home, my boys would have had my back. But in Bluford's gym, I was alone. Almost.

"You okay?" said a voice from behind

me. I looked up to see Eric. He offered his hand to help me up.

"That's it," I said, grabbing his arm. As soon as I got up, I headed straight to the locker room.

"Let it go," Eric said, following me.

Many kids were already lined up to go home, and they stared at me as I stormed in. They were the ones too scared to confront Steve even though they knew he was a jerk.

I heard Steve's laughter as I neared the section where my locker was. My blood was boiling.

"I don't care what he looks like, Clarence. That dude can transfer back to Zamora for all I care. He don't belong in this school anyway. He's the dumbest kid in my English class," he said.

Clarence cackled loudly, like he had never heard something funnier.

"Martin, don't do it," Eric whispered. He was right behind me.

"Stay out of my way," I said. Nothing would stop me.

Steve spotted me approaching him. I moved right into his face before the others even saw me.

"Oh you comin' back for more, Looney?" he said, trying to play cool.

Again, Clarence snorted.

I knew neither of them expected me to come back. They were used to people backing off.

Steve stepped forward, that big grin wider than ever. He was performing for the people in the locker room. "You got something to say?" he said. He was easily six inches taller than me. Probably had thirty pounds more muscle too.

But he wasn't smart. His hands were down, and I was close. It all happened so quickly that Steve didn't have a chance to react.

I sent an uppercut hammering into his jaw. The blow was strong enough to knock Steve back against his locker with a crash that sounded like a van smashing through the locker room.

"*Fight!*" someone yelled.

People began jumping over benches and scrambling to get a good view of us. It was the same thing that would happen in Zamora. No matter how nice your school is, people always want to see a fight.

"Martin, stop! *Martin!*" I heard Mr. Dooling yell. Many hands gripped my shoulders. One of the kids that grabbed me was Clarence. He tried to hook my arms so I couldn't punch back.

"Get up, Steve. Get him!" someone yelled. The voice came from one of the kids who stood over me in the gym.

But Mr. Dooling stepped in between us, and another gym teacher pulled Steve away from me.

"Boy, you're done," Steve said, wiping his hand against his swollen lip. "You are *done*!"

"Both of you are done," Mr. Dooling said. "Let's go. We're going to the principal's office. Now. Move!"

"But I have football practice," Steve begged.

"Well, that's something you can talk with Ms. Spencer about," Mr. Dooling said.

"But he didn't even do anything, Mr. Dooling," Clarence said. "Steve was just standing here, and this guy comes over and punches him."

"Tell that to Principal Spencer, not me. Come on."

Mr. Dooling and the teacher dragged us through the crowded hallways. People were rushing to go home, but many stopped to watch Steve and me being pulled to the main office. It was like we were criminals being arrested in public.

Once when I was a kid, my mom and I were outside of McDonald's when a bunch of undercover police surrounded a car and dragged the driver out. Everybody at the restaurant rushed out to watch as the guy was taken away in a squad car.

"They're taking the bad man away, *mijo*," my mother had said to me. Now I was one of the bad people. I could almost hear my mother's voice as she got the call from the principal's office.

Don't throw your life away, she'd say. And no matter how many times I would explain that it wasn't my fault, that Steve hit me, she wouldn't believe me. Neither would the principal. I was sure of that. I guess I can't blame them, but it still ain't right.

We turned a corner and headed down the main corridor that led to the office. Up ahead, looking right at us, were Vicky and Teresa. My face burned when I saw Vicky. She saw my reaction and raised her hand to her mouth in concern.

I'm not going to lie to you. I've been in trouble in school many times. Back in the day, it was cool to get yelled at by teachers. We all used to laugh about it.

No big deal. But when I saw Vicky, I felt embarrassed. I wished she'd never seen me like that.

"Do you believe me now, Vicky?" Teresa said as I passed. "I told you he's no good."

I wanted to argue with her, but what could I say? A few seconds later I was staring at the steel door with the tiny sign that said "Main Office." Mr. Dooling brought us into a conference room where Steve and I had to wait in fake leather seats that made a hissing sound when we sat down on them. We waited for ten minutes while Mr. Dooling and the principal talked in private.

"They're gonna bust you, man. You're outta here," Steve whispered at one point. I notice the office staff watching us, so I just bit my tongue.

"All right, Ms. Spencer is ready to see you, Steve," said Ms. Bader, the secretary in the office. Maybe it's me, but I could swear she smiled at him and frowned at me at the same time.

After ten minutes, Steve emerged with a wide grin on his face. "Bye, Ms. Spencer. I promise we'll win on Saturday," he said as he passed me.

"Go on in, Martin," Ms. Bader said.

An L-shaped desk with an old computer and stacks of papers sat in one corner of the office. A row of file cabinets lined the wall next to the desk. In the corner on the opposite side of the room was a small circular table with four chairs around it. A box of tissues and a pen rested on the table. I bet it was a place people did a lot of crying. Mostly parents, I'm sure.

In the middle of the room was a skinny woman with wire-rimmed glasses and lips so tight her mouth looked like the thin scar on Frankie's stomach. I knew I was in trouble.

"Hello, Martin. I'm Ms. Spencer. Just have a seat at the table," she said, grabbing a file from the cabinet and reading it quickly.

I slumped in the chair, grabbed the pen, and started clicking it. I was nervous.

"What's the problem between you and Steve Morris?" she asked. Her eyes focused on my face like she was looking for evidence of a crime. Like I told you at the beginning, I wasn't going to rat out Steve. Where I come from, you don't do that, even when you probably should.

"Nothin'," I said.

"Then why did you punch him?" I could hear an edge to her voice.

"It wasn't like that," I said. "We were just playing around, that's all."

"Martin, I've got Mr. Dooling and three other students who say you went up and punched Steve in the face. Now either you tell me everything that happened, or I am going with what they tell me."

"Look, Ms. Spencer. Me and Steve don't get along. He pushed me around in gym class, and I was just getting him back, that's all."

"By punching him in the face?" The edge to her voice got even sharper. She could almost cut you open with it if she wanted to.

I knew I was going down for the count, but I couldn't stop it. There was no way I could explain to her everything that led me to hit Steve. Even if I could tell her somehow, I could see she wasn't ready to hear it. Her tight jaw told me she was going to punish me no matter what I said.

"He was asking for it, Ms. Spencer. He pushed me first."

"No one reported this to me, Martin. Do you have any proof?"

I leaned back in the chair and dropped the pen on the table. Ms. Spencer watched me closely, stopping only to jot notes onto a pad of yellow lined paper. I knew all the kids who were witnesses were Steve's friends on the football team. None of them would tell the truth. But then I remembered Eric. He had witnessed the whole thing, and he hated Steve. If Eric told her what he saw, maybe Ms. Spencer wouldn't punish me.

"Yes," I said, ready to tell her about Eric, but then I remembered how scared he was of Steve. If I mentioned his name, and he told her the truth, Steve and his friends would probably go after him. After all, the two lived on the same street. The thought of Eric getting bullied turned my stomach. I was not going to be the reason another person got hurt. No more of that.

"Well, who is it?" Ms. Spencer asked me. Her patience was almost gone. I could tell. The lecture was coming.

"Never mind," I said. "No one saw anything because it happened at the end of class."

"I see," she said, writing something down and then putting the note into a folder that she quickly closed. "Look,

Martin. I know you are new in this school and making a switch is difficult, but I can't have you hitting other students. I don't know what you experienced at Zamora, but you should know that at Bluford we do not tolerate that kind of behavior."

I wanted to get up and walk out. Ms. Spencer acted as if I didn't know that fighting in school was wrong. Of course I know! But where I come from, when someone hits you, you have to hit back, or everyone will start treating you like you're soft. Wherever he was, Steve had a sore jaw to remind him not to push me around.

"Yes, Ms. Spencer," I said, just so she would stop lecturing me.

"Now I see you have already missed a day of school, and now you're here for fighting. All this in one week. That's not a good sign, Martin. Is there something going on with you that I should know about? Are you having problems at home?"

"No." Why do they always accuse your mother when you screw up? My mother couldn't do more to keep me out of trouble.

"Okay, Martin. I'm going to say this

once as a warning to you. This is a good school, and we would love to have you here. But if you continue this behavior, you and I are going to have serious problems. Do you understand?"

"Yes, Ms. Spencer."

She then handed me some papers and gave me a one day in-school suspension and a Saturday detention with Mr. Mitchell. The mention of his name reminded me that I had missed my after-school detention with him for the second day in a row.

Great. More trouble.

"One last thing, Martin. I have to call your mother and let her know what is happening. I am going to want to meet with the two of you in my office next week."

I squirmed in my seat. I knew Mom would be heartbroken to learn how much trouble I had gotten in at Bluford in less than a week. It would just be more proof to her that I was ruining my life.

Why are you doing this, mijo? You're throwing your life away, I could just hear her saying. There would be more tears, more yelling.

What made the image so painful was

that it was true. I was really screwing up, and I couldn't seem to change it. Back home, I just didn't fit in with Frankie and the boys. At Bluford, I didn't belong either. No place felt right anymore.

"I told you he's no good," Teresa had said. Her words began to crawl under my skin like painful splinters. Even Vicky probably thought I was just a troublemaker from the hood.

What else was I?

Looking at Ms. Spencer's wire glasses, I couldn't answer that question. My problems weren't just about Frankie, Steve or Bluford. They were also about me.

Huero died in my arms on the street outside my friend's house. He was shot in the back of the head by a bullet meant for someone else. His blood ran through my fingers as I held him like I did when he was a baby. He was just an innocent kid who never hurt anyone, never stole anything, never got in any fights. Not like me.

I wasn't always nice to him, but I was still his favorite person.

Usually, I chased him away when I was with my friends. I did that the day he was shot. He was on his way home when the shooter came down the block. Huero was so brave, he tried to warn me of the danger. I know he was scared. I could see it in his eyes, and I tried to protect him. But I was too late.

Huero would still be alive if he didn't follow me that afternoon. I wish I could replay that whole day because I would do it all differently, but I can't. On that summer day, my little brother Huero died trying to protect me. Though he was just eight years old, he is the biggest hero I know. And now he's gone because of me. There are no other heroes in my life.

I wrote the words sitting in the small yellow cinderblock room next to the principal's office. It looked more like a jail cell than a school room. There was nothing else I could do during in-school suspension except work. The only break from the hum and flicker of the fluorescent lights was when Ms. Bader brought me lunch, a plate of macaroni and cheese, a tiny carton of milk, and a chocolate chip cookie.

The paragraphs I wrote for Mr. Mitchell's class were too painful for me to reread, but at least they distracted me from the conversation I had with my mother the night before.

"What am I gonna do with you?" my mom screamed when I told her about the in-school suspension I got for hitting Steve.

"There's nothing you can do, Ma," I said to her.

I could tell that she didn't believe me when I explained that Steve and his crew had ganged up on me. "He hit me first, Ma. I was just hitting him back," I said.

"There you go again. It's always somebody else's fault. Whenever you get in trouble, it's 'cause someone said something or did something. When are *you* going to take responsibility for your actions and stop blaming others for the things that happen? And no matter how much I try to help you, *mijo*, you keep making dumb choices. You're getting more like your father each day."

"Stop it, Ma," I said. It felt like she

just slapped me in the face. "I ain't nothing like him."

She stormed down the hall and left me alone in the living room.

A couple hours later, I was laying in my bed listening to her talking on the phone to one of her friends. Her voice carried through the thin walls of our new place, so I could hear exactly what she was saying.

"Pray for him, Sonia. I love him, but there is nothing more I can do to control him. It's like he wants to throw his life away." I heard her blow her nose and shift around in her bed. "Pray that I don't lose him," she said.

I stayed up looking through a box of old pictures of Huero and thinking that her prayers were already too late. Heuro was gone, and in a way, I think, so was I.

Chapter 8

Suddenly, I was kneeling on the sidewalk next to Frankie's car. Huero was in my arms, his eyes closed, blood on my hands. The trees around us looked like they had been dipped in a coating of silver. We were outside, but it was strangely quiet.

"No!" I screamed from the top of my lungs. My homeboys were nowhere to be found, but the LeMans was there shining more brightly then ever. Too brightly.

Then there was the sound of tires screeching. I turned to see the white sedan racing off. I slid my arms out from under my brother and started chasing the car. I ran for blocks, the car just ahead of me. I passed through my old neighborhood, past the graveyard, and then down the street that led past the

Golden Grill, the ice cream stand, all the way to Bluford. In front of the high school, the car stopped.

This was it! I realized. The chance I was waiting for. There was a pistol in my hand just like the one Frankie bought. It felt like it was part of me, an extension of my fingers, not a foreign object.

I moved up on the car now, the gun out in front of me aimed at the driver's window. The glass was tinted so I couldn't see inside. But then the door began to open.

The gun was steady in my hand. I pointed it just where the driver's head would be as the gap between the door and the car slowly widened. I saw a hand, then an arm, and then a shoulder. Finally a face.

It couldn't be. My eyes had to be lying. Please tell me they were.

The driver of the car was me. I was about to shoot myself.

"No!" I screamed again.

Suddenly, a crowd came out of the high school. They were all watching. Vicky. Teresa. Eric. Mr. Mitchell. Officer Ramirez. Principal Spencer. My mother. They began to point at me, their faces angry and cruel. I felt hands grabbing me as I screamed for my life.

"It's okay. It's okay, *mijo*," I heard. It was my mother's voice. She was shaking me. I was in bed covered in sweat. "You're dreaming. That's all."

I had nightmares as a boy, especially around the time my father left, but they had stopped years ago. And even when they woke me up at night, I would usually forget them after a few minutes. They would just melt away like ice left in a glass on a hot day. But not this nightmare. It's like a picture frozen permanently in my brain. Whenever I think of it, I get the chills.

"Go back to sleep," she said after a few minutes.

I tried, but I didn't sleep more than a few hours that night.

On Saturday morning, I crawled out of bed as soon as I heard the alarm blaring. My head ached, and I could hear my mother making coffee in the kitchen. When she saw me, neither of us said a word. Her eyes were swollen and puffy, and I could see she hadn't slept much either.

She looked older to me, too. It was like she had aged five years since Huero died. I knew I was to blame for that too. Did you ever look in the mirror and just hate what you saw? That was me. I just couldn't stand to be in my own skin.

I ate a quick bowl of cereal and slipped out the door without saying goodbye. A few minutes later, I was outside of Bluford. A few workers were busy putting stripes on the football field as I approached. A handwritten poster was attached to the fence outside the football field. I could read the words easily from far away.

Bluford vs. Zamora
Today at 10:00

I knew Steve was somewhere nearby, getting ready for the game. I never cared about football before, but I wanted Zamora to pound Bluford into the dirt. Anything to stop Steve from bragging in class. It was bad enough that the guy got away with hitting me, that no one, not the principal, not even my own mother, would believe my side of the story. But if I had to watch Steve win on top of everything else, I'd just throw up. I'm serious.

My detention was scheduled to go

from 9:00 until 12:00, so I'd miss much of the game, but I could still check out the end. Maybe I'd get lucky and Zamora would win. Yeah, right.

Inside, the school was nearly empty except for a few janitors who ignored me as I passed them. I went straight to the room on the form that Ms. Spencer had given me, number 127, and grabbed a spot in the third row. The back row of desks was crowded.

Mr. Mitchell was sitting at the front of the room when I arrived. A large stack of student papers was on his desk, and he was hunched over reading one of them. He was wearing jeans and a gray sweatshirt instead of his usual dress shirt. For once, he didn't have one of those stupid ties on. He almost looked like a normal person, not like a teacher.

Besides me, four boys and two girls were in detention. One of the boys was listening to an iPod and bobbing his head. Another had his head on the desk and his eyes closed. The girl closest to me smelled like an ashtray full of old burnt-out cigarette butts. Nasty. Except for the smell, I was glad there were so many people in the classroom. At least I was not the only scrub who got in trouble during the first week of school.

"Okay, everyone," Mr. Mitchell said, closing the door at 9:00 sharp. "Here's the deal. If you have work to do, you can work on it. If not, I have books and magazines you can read. What you cannot do is sleep or stare into space. Got it?"

The group mumbled, and I could hear the lazy zip and snap of backpacks and jackets being opened. I grabbed my English notebook.

Next, Mr. Mitchell took attendance. He called each name out loud and marked a piece of paper as each student responded. But for my name, he raised his eyebrows and looked up from the list. He even gave me this strange look.

"Martin Luna," he said as if he was disappointed. Like I was someone he expected more from. That just rubbed me the wrong way,

"Right here, Mr. Mitchell," I said, as if I was as thrilled to see him. Who was he kidding, acting like he cares? I didn't buy that. I knew he was just like everyone else. In his eyes, I was trouble, the kid who missed class twice in the first week, who caused a disturbance in his class and got suspended.

For the next three hours, I read through my school books and fought off sleep. It was the most school work I'd done at one time in years. I even rewrote my English essay just because I was bored. I added a paragraph about Huero, describing him and what he liked to do. It made me so sad, I had to stop several times so I could calm down. I wondered what Frankie was up to.

At one point, I heard the distant sound of people cheering outside. It was the football game. I imagined Steve fumbling the ball and everyone in the bleachers booing him. What can I say? I was bored.

By the time Mr. Mitchell said detention was over, I was tired. My butt hurt from sitting in the metal chair, and I needed to get out of the smelly room. I dropped my assignment on Mr. Mitchell's desk, and rushed for the door.

"Martin, can I talk to you?" he said just before I reached the hallway. I wanted to keep going, but there was no way I could pretend that I hadn't heard him. The other students were already out the door.

"I have to go, Mr. Mitchell," I said, trying to think of an excuse to get away.

"I have plans." I knew what was coming. He was going to lecture me about my behavior, my missed classes, and the detention I never served. I wasn't in the mood, but there was no way out.

"I only need a few minutes."

I sat back down in the desk in the center of the room, crossed my arms, and stared at a spot on the floor. He leaned back against the desk at the front of the room.

"Okay, Martin, you need to decide what you want to be, and you need to do it now."

"What?" I said.

"Well, you can be the smart student that I know you are capable of being, or you can keep following the path you are on and get yourself into serious trouble. What's it going to be?"

I sat up in the chair. I felt a knot tighten in my head and chest. *Smart student?* He was playing games with me.

"You tell me, Mr. Mitchell. You're the one that seems to know everything all the time."

"No, Martin, I don't know everything. I just know what you show me. Right now, I see a good kid who could go either way, and I don't want to lose you."

His words made me cringe. They were too much like my mother's. And he kept looking at me, making me feel like I was on display or something.

"Man, what is your problem?" I asked. "You're always on my case like you know me or something, but you don't know jack about me, Mr. Mitchell," I said, surprised at the emotion spinning like an engine running out of control in my chest.

"All right," he replied, without a pause. "Then how about *helping* me understand you."

I felt this tension behind my eyes like someone was squeezing my head.

"What for? I don't need nothing from you. I got this far on my own."

"Yeah, you did. But Martin, you're heading for trouble. It's only been a week, and you've been absent twice. You've been suspended, and I can see you are on edge all the time. I've taught long enough to see that on your face."

The pressure in my head increased, like I was a giant balloon being overfilled with air.

"Yeah, well, I ain't like other kids at this school. I hate it here. I never want-ed to come here, and if I could, I'd leave,"

I said, putting the palms of my hands against my forehead, trying to push away the headache that was beginning to boil in my skull.

"Is that why you are acting up in my class?"

"What do *you* think?" I said, glaring at him as if he was to blame for everything that had gone wrong. "I'm sure you have an explanation. Go ahead. Tell me what it is." I know he didn't cause my problems, but his questions were getting to me. It's like I was covered in gasoline, and he was throwing matches at my face.

"Martin, lots of people feel like—"

"But they're *not* like me, Mr. Mitchell!" I yelled, standing up from my desk and kicking a chair. It shot across the room and slammed into a wall, shattering the quiet in the near empty school. I just couldn't control myself. I was just so angry. And Mr. Mitchell was just trying to set me off.

"Everything okay?" A janitor asked, opening the door and peering into the classroom. His eyes locked on me for a second. I knew he could see I was upset. "I heard something crash in here, and I thought I should check it out."

"Everything's fine, John," Mr. Mitchell said. "Thanks."

The janitor looked at the two of us before closing the door. I took a deep breath and swallowed back the emotion that made me snap.

"Why are you so angry, Martin?"

In that instant, I hated Mr. Mitchell. He just kept coming at me, making me think when I just wanted to stop. I didn't know if he was serious, and I didn't care if he was trying to help. There was just too much swirling in my head, a tangle of Huero, of my mother, of Frankie, of Steve, of Bluford, and of home. Mr. Mitchell was the least of my problems, yet it was like he was trying to make himself the center.

"I gotta go," I said, walking toward the door.

He stepped toward the door as if he was going to try to stop me.

"Stay outta my way, Mr. Mitchell. I don't wanna do something stupid, but you are pushing me. I need to go," I said. I swear I didn't want to hurt him. I never did anything to a teacher before, but I was losing it. I had to get outside.

Mr. Mitchell's eyes widened, and he still had that concerned look on his face.

But he stopped in his tracks. "Go ahead, Martin," he said.

I flung open the door and rushed out of Bluford. By the time I made it outside, my hands were trembling and my face was sweating. It felt like I had just been in a fist fight. I even had that same guilty feeling. At least I didn't hit anyone. I know that doesn't sound like a lot, but when you are me, you take what you can get.

As soon as I made it down the front steps to Bluford, I heard the people cheering from behind the high school. The football game. I'd almost forgotten.

I circled around the back of the school and walked up to the fence that kept neighborhood kids from playing on the field. The bleachers were about half full. Many of the people there were older, probably the parents of the players.

"Go on in and grab a seat," said a guard near me. "It's a good game."

Inside the fenced area, I couldn't believe what I saw. Though the buildings outside were a bit run down, Bluford's football field was in great shape, almost like what you'd expect in the suburbs or something. As I got near the bleachers, I could see the entire crowd was focused on the game. Some people were on their feet yelling.

"That was pass interference," an older man yelled. "Open your eyes, ref!"

In the front row, I saw a group of students. Some I recognized from my classes. Others were complete strangers.

I stepped up onto the bleachers and found a seat in the fourth row. The scoreboard was just to my right. Bluford was ahead 13 to 10. There were just three minutes left. Zamora had the football. Maybe Bluford would lose!

Surrounded by the crowd, I couldn't help but remember the last time I sat outside at a sporting event. It was late spring, when Huero was playing Little League baseball. Me and my mom had gone to all his games. We used to cheer for him whenever he did anything. We were so loud! Even though he was little, Huero could really swing a bat. The last time he was up, he hit a home run, and my mother and I hugged. It was only months ago, but it seemed like a different lifetime, one that could never have existed.

My eyes watered as I squinted under the bright sun to see the game. I must have missed several plays.

Zamora had brought the football all the way down to the Bluford five-yard line. The people around me were tense.

"You gotta stop 'em here, Coop!" yelled a girl in front of me. I recognized her face from school. I think her name was Tarah.

I couldn't believe what happened next. Somehow, the quarterback from my old school darted in for a touchdown. I cheered like football actually meant something to me. At least Steve Morris would stop boasting. People stared at me as if I was cursing at them or something, but I didn't care. It was like the game let me vent what I had been thinking for a week, that Bluford was hard, that I didn't like it, that I didn't belong, that no move could ever replace what I lost.

But there was still a minute left in the game.

On the kickoff, a player from Bluford caught the ball and sprinted up the field. He evaded two tackles, ran and stopped, dodged and weaved. Once, he seemed to pass through two other people trying to grab him, and at another point, he jumped completely over a Zamora tackler.

"Look at that boy run," said one of the girls in front of me. "He's gonna run like that all the way to college."

"The only thing faster than his feet is his mouth," replied Tarah.

Finally, only Zamora's kicker was between the Bluford runner and the end zone. The runner lowered his shoulder and plowed through the kicker as if he was made of paper.

Touchdown. Game over. Bluford won.

And then I saw who had the ball. It was Steve Morris.

I cursed out loud. You know the words.

Chapter 9

The crowd started leaving as soon as the game ended. Many people had big silly grins on their faces, but not me. I just wanted to get out of there. I climbed to the bottom of the bleachers and waited for the people to scatter.

"Martin! I can't believe you're here," said a cheerful, familiar voice.

I turned to see Vicky standing next to me. I hadn't seen her since Mr. Dooling dragged me through the hallway to Ms. Spencer's office. I felt a little embarrassed. Not far away were Teresa and another girl I didn't know. Teresa looked at me as if I had just mugged her mother.

"Hi, Vicky," I said, trying to hide my surprise. "Don't tell me you're a football fan! What about all the winner-loser stuff?" I teased.

She smiled, and I swear my whole day got better. There was just something about her eyes and the way the long waves of her hair curled against her neck and face. "Don't worry, Martin. Believe me, there are many places I'd rather be. But Teresa likes this guy on the team, and she made me promise to sit with her while she watched him. What about you?"

I didn't want her to know the truth, but I couldn't bring myself to lie to her. "I had a Saturday detention with Mr. Mitchell. I just got out," I said, expecting her to walk away. I could see Teresa watching us through the crowd. She looked more annoyed than ever, glaring at Vicky as if no one else could see her face. "Vicky, I think Teresa wants you or something," I said.

"She's so rude sometimes," Vicky snapped, her eyes flashing with anger. "I'll be right back." I watched as the girls talked and Teresa rolled her eyes. That girl hated me. Some people are just like that. Vicky came back a minute later, while Teresa walked away with her friend. "Sorry about that."

"Look, if you need to go, it's cool."

"No, Martin, I want to talk to you,"

she said. She was so serious I almost turned around to make sure she was talking to me. I'd never met a girl like her back home. "I heard about what happened in the gym with you and Steve. I just want you to know that what he did was wrong."

The girl stunned me. She seemed angry *for* me, but not *at* me. Like she was on my side. I wasn't sure what to say. "Yeah, well, someone needs to tell Ms. Spencer that."

"Don't worry. I will on Monday," she said.

"Girl, you're crazy," I said, shaking my head at her. She was a fighter. I could see that, but I didn't understand why she was talking to me.

"You're not the first person to say that," she said proudly.

"Well I don't know if I should be talking to you then. My mother always told me to watch out for the crazy girls."

"Yeah, well my mother always tells me to watch out for the dangerous boys."

"Oh, so I'm dangerous now?" I said, acting hurt.

"I don't think so, but that's not what Teresa says," she replied with a grin that convinced me that she was smarter than any of my other friends, even Frankie. She was quiet for several seconds, and we passed the crowd from Bluford and made our way into the neighborhood. "You wanna take a walk to the park?"

My heart skipped a beat. I couldn't believe she wanted to spend time with me. "*Now*?" I said.

"Or we could stay here and wait for Steve," she replied.

"Let's do that," I said, pretending to be serious.

"C'mon." She gave me a playful punch in the stomach as we started walking.

I don't know how it happened, but Vicky and I spent the whole afternoon together. It was like beauty and the beast or something. Here was Vicky, this smart girl, an A student, with great olive skin, the whitest smile, black spiraled hair stretching down her back, and eyes that seem to peer right into your soul. And then there's me, Martin Luna. You know my deal.

For a while, we just talked about Bluford. She asked me a lot of questions about school and told me things about some of the people in our English class. At one point I mentioned Mr. Mitchell, and she turned to me.

"Mr. Mitchell is the best, Martin," she said. "He can be tough, but he's fair, and he cares about what happens to people around here. He even grew up in the neighborhood."

I started to tell her that I thought he was too nosy, and she stopped me.

"He asks a lot of questions because he cares. I heard that last year, he showed up at some kid's house to warn the parents that their son was using drugs. He's like that. Always trying to help." I wasn't about to tell her that I nearly lost it during detention and almost hit him.

"His ties are bad," I said, trying to change the subject.

"Yeah, he needs help with his clothes. My mom says he needs a woman in his life. My dad just laughs about it." Of course, she had both her parents at home.

We left the park and went to Niko's for pizza. The place was crowded with people from Bluford. Two tables away, Cooper and that girl Tarah were sitting with a few other students. One of them was Darcy from my English class.

"All Steve has to do is start talking and everyone else runs away," I heard Cooper say out loud between fits of laughter. "That's why no one tackles him. I'm serious."

"Yeah, but you're lucky he's on your team, Coop," Tarah said.

I nodded to him as I got a slice of my favorite pizza, extra cheese and pepperoni, and a plain slice for Vicky. As we ate, she told me that Teresa used to like a guy who delivered pizza for Niko's.

"That girl hates me," I said.

"No. She doesn't hate you. She just doesn't trust you," Vicky said, raising her eyebrows.

I still couldn't figure her out. I had no idea why she looked at me so seriously. "What about you?" I just had to ask.

"I'm not sure yet," she said.

It was like she took a spoon, shoved it into my chest, and started stirring me like I was a pitcher of iced tea. I was so confused. I wanted to be the kind of guy she could trust, someone that deserved her, but I didn't know what that was.

Everything I knew about girls I learned from Frankie. Back home, he always had girls chasing him. They were pretty, but they always seemed like they were trying to get away from something. One had a kid already. Might even have been Frankie's, though he would never say. Vicky was totally different from all that. I knew she wouldn't like Frankie, so I couldn't understand why she was talking to me.

"Vicky, you and me, we're different from each other," I said, not knowing where I was going but unable to stop. "Really different."

"*So*," she said. "What's that mean?"

"I don't know. It just seems like . . . you shouldn't be here with me." It might have been the most honest thing I said since Huero died. I couldn't even look at her. It hurt.

She touched my hand then just for a second before taking it back. "Martin, when I first saw you I was like, 'Oh no, who is this boy acting so hard?' But when you wrote about your brother, you seemed so sad. That's when I decided I wanted to talk to you."

"Oh, so you feel sorry for me?" That explained it. I was a charity project for her.

"No, it's not like that," she said, staring me down. "It's just . . . I don't know.

It's like you're more real than the guys around here."

"What?"

"Look at Steve. He seems like he has it all together. He's popular. He's got a great body, and he plays football. But then when you talk to him, he's a complete jerk. You're the opposite. From the outside, you seem like you'd be mean, but you're not. Not at all."

I didn't know what to say. I mean, I know she was trying to be nice, and I was happy she was talking to me. But I just had to flag what she said.

"What's wrong with my body?"

"Nothing," she said and then blushed. "*No.* That's not the point." She shook her head and pulled her hair back behind her ear. "Steve and I went out for three months, and he never said anything nice to me about my grandmother even when I told him about her. You knew me for two minutes, and you said something that was so nice."

There was this little crease in her forehead as she spoke, a perfect fold that was there because she was concentrating to get the right words out. I wanted to touch her face, to thank her somehow, but I couldn't move. I could barely speak. What was happening to me?

Frankie would have slapped me if he'd seen me.

You're losin' it, homes, he'd say. *No girl is as important as us, your family.*

But for the first time, I almost didn't care.

On Sunday, I went to church with my mother. Don't ask me why.

My mother looked at me like I had a fever when she saw me in my dress shirt waiting for her in the living room.

"You're coming to Mass with me?" she asked. She didn't even blink once as she spoke to me.

"Yeah, why?" I said. I didn't want to make a big deal about it.

"Nothing, *mijo,*" she said, smiling slightly and leading me to the car.

"Good to see you again, Martin," one older woman said, patting my back as soon as I walked into the church.

"You look so handsome," said another.

Their wide eyes and long stares told me they were some of the people my mom called when she needed to talk about me.

I hadn't been to church since Huero's funeral, but the sweet, smoky scent of incense brought me right back to the moment Huero was in his coffin in front of the altar. I was so angry then. The memory is as sharp as a switch-blade. While the priest spoke against gang violence, I was planning it.

But now the whole thing was muddy and confusing. Just thinking about it made my head pound and my heart race, and I could barely follow the priest's talk on forgiveness.

Afterwards we stopped at Huero's grave. The rose I had left was still there, the petals already beginning to wilt and dry.

"I miss him, *mijo*," said my mom as we stood there together, her tears falling silently to the ground in front of the headstone.

"Me too, Ma," I said, putting my arm on her shoulder. She leaned into me and began to sob, and I held her weight. It felt like she would collapse without me.

See me after class.

That's the only comment Mr. Mitchell wrote on my English assignment. It was Monday morning, and after everything, I was trying my best to take Bluford seriously. I got to school on time, and even though I wanted to skip English, I dragged myself into Mr. Mitchell's class and tried to pretend that the Saturday detention incident never happened.

Vicky was acting strange all of a sudden, and that was bothering me too. When she came to class, she was almost yelling at Teresa.

"I *had* to tell her," Vicky said, her voice louder than usual.

"You should have stayed out of it, Vic," Teresa answered and then spotted me. Her mouth snapped shut like the mousetraps we used to use in our kitchen.

Before I could say anything, Mr. Mitchell walked in, and Vicky gave me this weak smile which told me something was wrong. The only good thing was that Steve was absent for the first half of class, so I didn't have to hear him brag about Saturday. That would have set me off.

When he finally came in, he had this scowl on his face like he was ready to hit somebody. I didn't care. Everyone watched him, including Mr. Mitchell, but no one said anything.

I wanted to talk to Vicky at the end of class, but Mr. Mitchell's note meant I had to see him instead. I knew he was going to tell me all the things I did wrong on the assignment. At least at Zamora, I could get a C for not even trying. Here I tried my best, and I was going to fail.

"You said I had to see you," I said as soon as the bell rang, bracing myself for bad news.

"Yes, Martin. First, I want to say I am sorry about Saturday. I really put you in a corner, and I didn't mean to do that. Sometimes the best thing we can do is to walk away from a situation that isn't good, and I am glad you did that and not something else."

The man was crazy. I am convinced of it. Teachers don't apologize! Not any that I know.

"Second, your essay was outstanding and powerful. It took a lot of courage to write it, and I am giving it an A. Good job. You may want to consider writing for the school paper, the *Bluford Bugler*. Let me know if this interests you."

I was speechless. Me? An A? Only Huero could make that happen.

"Finally, I am just going to repeat what I said on Saturday. Martin, you are talented, and you could have a bright future ahead of you. Don't throw it away. When you feel things getting out of hand, when you know you're getting over your head, talk to me. I'm here for you. I mean that."

I don't know what planet Mr. Mitchell came from, but maybe it wasn't such a bad place. I feel a little embarrassed admitting this, but I was like a little kid on Christmas Day. It was the first time I can remember a teacher saying something good about me—Martin Luna!

For the rest of the day, nothing could touch me, not the C I got on a biology quiz, not Mr. Dooling's watching my every move in the gym, not Steve staring at me in the locker room. Only Vicky kept it from being a perfect day. I had to find her.

"Is everything okay?" I asked, catching her as she walked out.

"I don't know, Martin," she said tensely. "You should go home." We descended the stairs together and headed down the street.

"Why? You sick of me already?"

"No. It's just that I told Ms. Spencer what happened with you. Someone else did too. Now Steve and some other guys on the football team are in trouble.

Teresa said you might be too."

"Why? What's Ms. Spencer gonna do to me?"

"It's not Ms. Spencer I'm worried about. It's you. Steve and his friends are up to something."

I almost laughed. "Please! I ain't scared of them. They ain't gonna touch me."

"I don't know, Martin," she said, looking over her shoulder. "Oh no."

A small black sedan passed us slowly on the other side of the street. There were three guys in the back seat, two in the front. I could see them turning their heads and saying something. One of them pointed at me. I had this sinking feeling, like the concrete beneath my feet had just gotten soft and sticky. Like the time just before Huero got shot.

The car did a U-turn in the middle of the street and looped back toward us. Steve was in the front seat.

Chapter 10

"Let's just keep walking," Vicky said. A slight tremor shook her voice.

The car moved closer, but I didn't budge. We couldn't run even if we wanted to. Bluford was almost two blocks behind us, and the only thing nearby was a grocery store across a wide parking lot. There was no way we could reach the store in time.

"C'mon, Martin," she insisted. She grabbed my arm, and pulled me into the lot toward the store. I could feel her nails digging into my skin.

It was like I was reliving the nightmare of the summer all over again. Another person was in the wrong place at the wrong time because of me. I'd lost my brother when he tried to warn me. I wasn't going to lose the girl who defended me to the principal.

"Vicky, there's no time. You gotta get away from me *now*," I said as the car squeaked to a stop. "*Go!*"

I started to shake. The air seemed to grow quiet. It was like I was talking to Huero.

"I can't just leave you here, Martin," she said.

I turned and put my hands on her shoulders. "Vicky, you have to go *now*! It's me they want, not you. *Go!*"

The car doors opened.

"I'm staying," she whispered bravely. "Who knows what they'll do if I leave."

If I had more time, I would have carried her to the safety of the grocery store myself, but suddenly there were five guys from the Bluford football team standing before us. Steve was in the front. I stepped in front of Vicky to face him.

"You sure know how to pick your friends, Vicky," he said, as he stared at me. "Why don't you go run for the border so me and Taco Boy here can talk."

The other guys started laughing. One of them was Clarence. The others I didn't recognize.

"What's your problem, Steve?" she

snapped. I couldn't deal with her defending me.

"One shot in the face wasn't enough for you, Steve?" I taunted. "Now you gotta bring out your boys 'cause you couldn't handle me yourself."

"Don't do this, Martin," Vicky said. "Please don't do this."

Steve's eyes narrowed, and he moved right into my face. My eyes were at the same height as his nostrils. I heard the other guys step in closer, forming a loose circle around us.

"We all got in trouble because of you," one of the guys said. "We're out of next week's game against Lincoln."

"Oh, so ganging up on Martin is gonna make things better?" Vicky said. "You probably won't play for years."

"Vicky, you should stay out of this. I heard you were one of the ones that ratted us out," Steve growled.

I couldn't let the attention turn toward her. "Yo, are we just gonna sit around here and talk all day, 'cause I got things to do," I said, giving Steve a tap on his chest to taunt him.

"Martin, don't!" she yelled.

Suddenly Steve shoved me. I stumbled a few steps and bumped against one of the other guys who pushed me right back toward Steve.

"Let's do this," Steve said, raising his fists.

"Go, Vicky!" I said. As long as she was safe, I wouldn't care what happened.

Steve's fists were up like a boxer's. With cat-like speed, he threw a punch at my head. If I hadn't been in plenty of fights back home, he would have caught me, but I dodged just in time.

Vicky watched in horror. I didn't want to fight in front of her. She didn't know that side of me, and I didn't want her to see it. I liked what she saw in me better. But Steve was giving me no choice.

"Go!" I yelled, avoiding another shot.

Just then a crushing blow hit me in the back. It came from Clarence, sending a hot streak of pain into me. I was okay, but I knew I couldn't fight on both sides. Still, Clarence's wide face was a big target, and I tagged him good on his right eye. He grunted and grabbed his face, moving out of the circle. But Steve and two others moved in. I was in trouble.

"Martin!" Vicky yelled.

Just then, I heard the thundery hum

and boom of a powerful sound system.

In the space behind Steve's shoulder, I spotted a car. It was deep blue and sparkling like the ocean under the bright sun. It rolled low to the ground, and its windows were tinted so dark that they appeared black. It was Frankie's LeMans!

The sound was so loud everybody stopped to look, and I saw Chago in my old spot, the passenger seat. He hollered something, and the Le Mans stopped. The football players turned around.

Frankie stepped out of the car with this sick sneer that twisted up like the scar on his stomach. Chago, Junie, Jesus were there too. And there was some other kid I didn't know. He seemed young. Maybe thirteen or fourteen. New blood to replace me.

"Hey, homes," Frankie barked. "You ain't havin' a party without us, are ya?" He then spit a nasty white glob on the ground right in front of Clarence's shoe.

"Who's that?" one of the football players whispered. They broke their circle around me and stood together nervously, leaving Steve in the front. There were six of us and five of them.

Frankie stood in front of Steve like he

138

was inspecting a beat-up car that was overpriced. I can't imagine what Steve was thinking, facing this older guy with tattoos, scars, and not a trace of fear in his eyes.

"Know what?" Frankie said, glaring at Steve, who was silent. "I don't think I like the guest list. What are you looking at?"

Frankie shoved him before he could answer. If not for Steve's quick feet, he would have gone down right there. Clarence started to move in to defend Steve, but then Junie pulled out a switchblade. Everyone stood frozen in place. It was like I never left home.

I knew exactly what was gonna happen next. I knew it like a rerun that you've seen on TV fifteen times. Frankie would tear Steve up, hurt him, make him bleed, and we would watch. It was going to be an ugly scene from my old world thrown into my new one. Maybe it would be worse. Frankie had this hungry glint in his eye. He was always looking for a reason to show how tough he was. Steve gave him an excuse to hurt what he hated most, a cocky kid who didn't need the street to be successful.

It would be a huge story in school

too. Maybe in the papers. "Star Running Back Hurt in Gang Assault." I'd be a famous criminal at Bluford.

Steve must have known what was coming. He was sweating, and his eyes darted back and forth. He looked like a scared animal caught in a trap.

"You're not scared, are you?" Frankie said, circling Steve, who seemed smaller somehow. He turned to his friends for an answer, but they were as frightened as he was. One of them was trembling like he had a chill or something.

I just couldn't do it. Call me soft, or a wimp. But I couldn't just stand there and watch. I felt dirty.

Frankie moved in for his first strike. "What's the matter?" he said, stepping close. He was going to hurt Steve bad. I could see it like I could see the fear on Steve's face. All of Bluford would hate me. Everything Teresa said would be right. I had to do something.

"Back off, Frankie," I urged. "It's all right. We're cool."

Frankie looked me square in the face. "*What?*"

The new young kid in Frankie's posse looked outraged. I could see he was trying to impress Frankie.

"Just leave him alone," I said, staring at the new kid. He had to be just a few years older than Huero. He didn't belong there seeing all this.

"What are you talkin' about?" Frankie said. "Some fool messes with one of my own, I get in his face."

"Not this time, Frankie. He ain't worth it." Before Frankie could do anything, I stepped in between him and Steve. "Go, Steve. All of you, get outta here." They didn't hesitate. In seconds, they were in their car and rolling away. Little boys running back to Mom.

Frankie turned to me and started shouting. "What's going through your mind, homes? If we didn't come here lookin' for you, you'd a got beat down. We saw how that dude was *pushin'* you around. How could you just stand there and take it?"

"Yeah!" said Junie. "That's not the Martin we remember."

I couldn't explain it myself. Frankie was watching me again. Like he did the other day when I was at his house. The new kid fidgeted uneasily. "I just got a lot going on, you know. I'm thinkin' about a lot of things."

"Dudes," I heard Junie mutter just

above a whisper. "He's still messed-up in the head."

Like that boy had room to talk. His eyes were pink from smoking weed. It was his favorite thing to do.

"Well, we got something else for you to think about, homes." Frankie said, nodding to Chago.

"We found the punk who shot Huero," Chago said. "We figured everything out. The where, the who, and the how. That's why we were lookin' for you. Everything's going down tomorrow morning. We'll pick you up right here at 9:00. "

"You're still down, right, Martin?" Frankie said.

I almost passed out. They did it. They had finally found the person who took my brother. I still had the rage, the hunger. It was mixed with other things, but it was still there. It still is. And it spoke for me.

"Yeah, I'll be here," I said.

Frankie smiled and nodded. "We'll see you then, homes." He said.

He and the boys made their way back to the car. "9:00, homes. Be ready!" said the kid, whoever he was. Little punk didn't even know Huero, but there he was rolling up with the big boys.

A second later, the Le Mans tore off, and I was standing at the edge of the parking lot alone. Then I remembered something. *Vicky.* She was gone.

She must have slipped away when Frankie showed up. That meant she'd seen my crowd and knew what we were like.

I had lost her. Probably for good. But I was about to lose everything.

"Your English teacher, Mr. Mitchell, called me this afternoon. He said you got an A on your first paper, and he told me you wrote about Huero. Why didn't you say anything to me?" my mother said when she got home from work. It was almost 10:00. She was about to weep again, but this time she was happy.

"It's no big deal, Ma," I said. Just looking at her was torture.

"We talked for a while about you. He seems like a good man."

"He's all right." I walked to my room. "I'm tired," I said.

"I am so glad you're turning things around. My prayers are being answered. My baby got an A," she said as I closed the door, her voice full of pride. But she

143

had no clue what I was about to do. Neither did I.

That was last night.

I spent ten hours staring at the ceiling, imagining how this morning would play out. But you can make all the plans in the world and never really know what's going to happen. Huero's death taught me that.

When I got up, I threw my gear on, my baggy pants, my boots, my bandanna, and I headed out. I couldn't eat nothing. My stomach was doing cartwheels as I made my way toward Bluford.

The LeMans was waiting in the parking lot next to where we'd almost fought the day before. Its engine growled in the crisp morning air. Frankie and Chago were standing in front of the car. Frankie was smoking.

"See! I told you he would come," Chago said.

"Check it out. He's got his bandanna with him, homies. Martin's back," said Junie through the open window.

I marched straight up to Frankie.

"Good to see you, homes," he said.

"What's the deal?"

"Dude's name is Hector Maldonado.

He lives behind that park where I got stabbed. At 10:00, he's gonna try and go to work, but he ain't gonna get there," Frankie said with a chuckle.

There had to be a reason. Frankie always knew more than he said. I'd gotten used to that now. So I had to think around him. When I was up all night thinking about what we were about to do, one question kept coming back to me.

"Why was this guy shooting at us this summer, Frankie?" I had to ask it.

Frankie spat on the ground. He always hated when we asked him questions. He still did. "Don't matter. He still shot your brother, right?"

My hands were tingling, and there was sweat pouring down my neck. It was like he slapped me in the face. Frankie's response set my mind spinning.

"C'mon. Let's go, homies," Chago said. "Martin, you got your old seat, man." He moved to the back of the Le Mans, letting me sit in the front next to Frankie. I was number two again.

"Check under your seat," Frankie said to me as we got into the car and he revved the engine. I reached down and touched the smooth cold metal of a gun.

Of course. Frankie had made sure we each had guns. Now everyone was armed. Everyone except him. It was all making sense. Too much sense.

The car started to roll forward.

Behind me, in the rearview mirror, I could see a section of the fence that protected Bluford. In front of me was the busy street that would lead us away. I sat in between, wearing my gear, ready to do something I could never take back. I was standing on the edge of a knife.

Frankie pulled the LeMans to the end of the lot. A bus waiting in traffic blocked us from making our turn. We were quiet. Frankie took a drag from his cigarette, and a coil of smoke snaked up from his face. His jaw was tight, and he was tapping on the steering wheel, avoiding eye contact with me. The crowded car stank like sweat and cigarettes.

I knew why Frankie hadn't answered my question. I'd known it for days now. Knew it all night as I thought of a plan. Knew Frankie would never tell. He was too smart to give out information that could bust him, but I knew the truth.

Huero was shot because of Frankie. Someone was trying to take Frankie out, probably because he had done something horrible. And now Frankie was using us to clean up his mess, take out his enemies. Arming us to make him stronger. Bringing in new blood to give him more muscle. Waiting until he was sure we could do things right. Making us pull the trigger while he sat back and watched. We were his pawns.

And if we got busted, he could deny everything. Maybe even let us take the fall for him. Frankie's like that when he has to be.

Truth is, we'd only be creating another mess. Another broken family. Another crying mother. Another plot to collect tears in a graveyard. Another headstone in a growing sea of graves.

Not me. Not Martin Luna. Not anymore.

"There's just too many dead people," Huero had said. My little brother was right. He taught me. There had to be another way. I thought of one. Even if it was a long shot, I had to try it.

I opened the car door.

"Whatcha doin', Martin?" Chago asked.

"Leaving." I stepped out and started walking to Bluford.

Frankie whipped the LeMans around

in front of me and got out.

"Homes, you know you can't leave us," he said. "Now get in the car."

"I'm not doin' it, Frankie. I'm serious."

"*Get in the car*, Martin." His voice was cold. Like a frozen dagger.

The car emptied. All my old homeboys got out to watch me challenge Frankie. I know deep inside all of them had wished they could do it at some point, but they were too scared.

"I'm out," I said, trying to walk around him.

Frankie sidestepped, grabbed my shirt, and moved into my face. "Don't make me do this, homes."

I shoved him back out of my face, and he came back with two lightning-fast punches to my side. The second one hit like a hammer, and I felt a tearing pain as I backed away. It was my ribs. Another hit like that and I'd be on the ground. I hunched over against the pain.

Frankie stepped back. It was what he always did when he fought someone. I'd seen it many times. I think he did it to check the damage. At least he was predictable.

"Get in the car now," Frankie

ordered.

"I'm out!"

Frankie circled in on me again, looking for an opening. I knew his style. I had planned for it. There was no way I could beat him in a fight, especially not if the boys joined in. Hitting back would only feed Frankie's fire. He might kill me. I had to fight him another way.

The fists came again. I blocked and dodged what I could, but the third hit caught me across the chin, spinning my head and splitting my lip.

"You're coming with us, Martin," Frankie growled. "One way or the other."

"No, Frankie. It's over."

Frankie charged like an animal. He was just too fast. In seconds, he hit me repeatedly, opening a cut above my eye, bruising my arms, my jaw, my lip. It was like the last year before Mom got the restraining order against my dad. It was a repeat of the time I became part of Frankie's gang. I knew how to take a beating. But you can only take it for so long before your legs get weak, you get dizzy, and you fall.

I went down on my knees.

"C'mon, Martin. We're family, man. Brothers," Chago said. "Let's go."

"My brother was Huero, Chago, and he's dead because of something Frankie did. You know it's true. What we are about to do, it ain't family, Chago. It's crazy."

Frankie went to the car and came back a second later. I knew he had one of the guns. It was in his hand, concealed in his coat pocket so passing traffic couldn't see it.

"You can't leave your family, Martin," Frankie said. He knew I had spotted the gun. We all did.

"Oh, no. Don't do this, Frankie," Chago said. "Just let it go, man."

"My brother's death wasn't enough for you, huh, Frankie? Now you wanna take me too? You might as well kill my mother too. Three lives. Is that what you call family, Frankie?"

He stood over me, the gun inches from my head. No one said a word. But Chago kept shaking his head. Junie kept eyeing the street.

Frankie had the gun, but I played the only cards I had. He'd probably kill me if I fought him. He'd hunt me if I ratted him out. The only way out was to show him I had nothing to lose. It was a language Frankie understood. Years growing up together taught me that.

"I can't go no further. Do what you gotta do."

Even Frankie had a sliver of heart left. He knew I had lost my brother because of him. He knew I was serious and that he couldn't change my mind. He shook his head.

"This ain't done," he said, looking at me and lowering the gun. Without another word, he jumped into the LeMans, and the boys followed. An instant later, he gunned the accelerator, and the car pulled away in a cloud of white tire smoke. I was alone on my knees. A free man with nothing.

Did I run from my old life? I guess you could say that. I ran before it swallowed me whole, and I ended up where I was heading. Jail or dead. A little obituary in the back of the newspaper. A nobody. A nothing. I want more than that. Sometimes you gotta run.

But what now? I don't know. My old world's been ripped away, and the new one doesn't make much sense. It's just me, this big school, a stubborn girl, a new neighborhood, and the words of my crazy teacher, Mr. Mitchell.

Martin, you are talented, and you could have a bright future ahead of you. Don't throw it away. When you feel things getting out of hand, when you know you're getting over your head, talk to me. I'm here for you. I mean that.

I'm holding onto those words like a lifeline.

So here I am out in front of Bluford three hours late. The guard is coming out to meet me. So is Ms. Spencer. I know they can see the blood. I got a lot to explain, and I know she's not going to believe me. But I'll try. I made my choice. I gotta live with it.

I ain't no killer. No one in my family is. That's how it's going to stay.

The guard is almost here. They'll take me to the office. I'll make a phone call to my mom and Officer Ramirez. I got the name of the person who shot my brother.

Rest in peace, Huero. I'll make you proud.

"I can't do this again, Carl. I don't have the strength, not without Mama."

Darcy Wills hid in the dark hallway listening to the sound of her mother's weary voice. It was 11:00 at night, and Mom was in the bedroom talking with Dad. Their door was closed. But through the thin walls of her family's small house, Darcy could hear them as if they were standing right in front of her.

"So what are you trying to say?" Dad asked. His voice was strained, as if he was carrying a heavy block of cement on his back.

Darcy stood still as a statue, careful not to make a sound that would alert her parents to the fact that she was just a few feet away in the dark.

"I don't know, Carl," Mom answered.

Find out what happens next at

BLUFORD HIGH

Summer of Secrets

A frightening ordeal at the end of the school year has turned Darcy Wills's world upside down. And her parents, distracted by problems at home, don't seem to notice her troubles. With her ex-boyfriend miles away in Detroit and her beloved grandmother gone, Darcy is more alone than ever. Darcy turns to her remaining friends, only to discover one of them has an even bigger secret. Now, forced into a crisis beyond her control, Darcy must take a stand for herself—and for her friend. When the dust settles, Darcy will never be the same again.

Turn the page for a special sneak preview. . . .

"I don't know anything anymore."

There was a moment of silence, and Darcy thought she heard her mother sob.

"I just don't have a good feeling about any of this."

So it *was* true, Darcy thought. Something was definitely wrong with her parents. Darcy had sensed it for days. She had noticed tension between them and had even heard Mom snap a few times, but until now she figured her mother was still recovering from the loss of Grandma.

Only three weeks ago, after a slow, steady decline in her health, Grandma had died in her sleep in the bedroom at the end of the hallway. The loss left a depressing void in the house. But in the three weeks that had passed, the sadness was replaced by an uncomfortable silence, one Darcy couldn't understand.

"Just don't worry about it, Darce," said her sister Jamee last week. Jamee was fourteen, two years younger than Darcy. "Anyway, it's none of your business. Besides, Mom's tough, and Dad's here. They'll be okay."

WELCOME TO BLUFORD HIGH.

IT'S NOT JUST SCHOOL—

IT'S REAL LIFE.